# WINE COUNTRY COURIER
*Community Buzz*

The beeswax candles were lit, the quartet was playing, the peach and ivory roses were exquisite…and if beneath the veil the bride was not whom we expected, well, no one was going to question the groom, millionaire Simon Pearce!

Despite the last-minute pinch-hitting, Mr. Pearce appeared unruffled and determined at his nuptials the other day. The bride, heiress Megan Ashton—the wedding coordinator—was resplendent in her silk white gown. The official word is that although it was a spur-of-the-moment decision to marry, the two had grown quite fond of each other over the past several weeks…as they planned Mr. Pearce's wedding to another woman!

Rest assured, dear readers, that whenever the Ashton name appears in print, a scandal is sure to follow. I can't wait to see what they have in store for *Courier* readers next!

Dear Reader,

Welcome to another scintillating month of passionate reads. Silhouette Desire has a fabulous lineup of books, beginning with *Society-Page Seduction* by Maureen Child, the newest title in DYNASTIES: THE ASHTONS. You'll love the surprises this dynamic family has in store for you…and each other. And welcome back *New York Times* bestselling author Joan Hohl, who returns to Desire with the long-awaited *A Man Apart,* the story of Mitch Grainger—a man we guarantee won't be alone for long!

The wonderful Dixie Browning concludes her DIVAS WHO DISH series with the highly provocative *Her Fifth Husband?* (Don't you want to know what happened to grooms one through four?) Cait London is back with another title in her HEARTBREAKERS series, with *Total Package.* The wonderful Anna DePalo gives us an alpha male to die for, in *Under the Tycoon's Protection.* And finally, we're proud to introduce author Juliet Burns as she makes her publishing debut with *High-Stakes Passion.*

Here's hoping you enjoy all that Silhouette Desire has to offer you…this month and all the months to come!

Best,

*Melissa Jeglinski*

Melissa Jeglinski
Senior Editor
Silhouette Desire

Please address questions and book requests to:
Silhouette Reader Service
U.S.: 3010 Walden Ave., P.O. Box 1325, Buffalo, NY 14269
Canadian: P.O. Box 609, Fort Erie, Ont. L2A 5X3

DYNASTIES: THE ASHTONS

# SOCIETY-PAGE SEDUCTION

## Maureen Child

Published by Silhouette Books
**America's Publisher of Contemporary Romance**

Special thanks and acknowledgment are given to Maureen Child for her contribution to the DYNASTIES: THE ASHTONS series.

To my mom, Sallye Carberry, for more reasons than I could possibly list here! I love you, Mom.

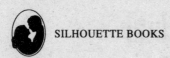 SILHOUETTE BOOKS

ISBN 0-373-76639-4

SOCIETY-PAGE SEDUCTION

Copyright © 2005 by Harlequin Books S.A.

Visit Silhouette Books at www.eHarlequin.com

Printed in U.S.A.

**Books by Maureen Child**

## MAUREEN CHILD

is a California native who loves to travel. Every chance they get, she and her husband are taking off on another research trip. The author of more than sixty books, Maureen loves a happy ending and still swears that she has the best job in the world. She lives in Southern California with her husband, two children and a golden retriever with delusions of grandeur.

Visit her Web site at www.maureenchild.com.

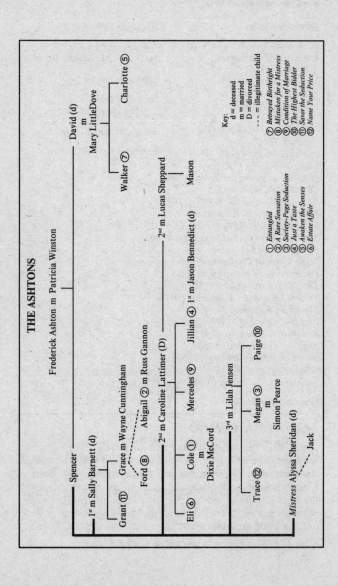

# THE ASHTONS

Frederick Ashton m Patricia Winston

Spencer

David (d)
m
Mary LittleDove

1ˢᵗ m Sally Barnett (d)

Grace m Wayne Cunningham

Abigail ② m Russ Gannon

Ford ⑧

2ⁿᵈ m Caroline Lattimer (D)

Walker ⑦        Charlotte ⑤

2ⁿᵈ m Lucas Sheppard

Mason

Grant ⑪

Jillian ④ 1ˢᵗ m Jason Bennedict (d)

Mercedes ⑨

Cole ①
m
Dixie McCord

Eli ⑥

3ʳᵈ m Lilah Jensen

Megan ③
m
Simon Pearce

Paige ⑩

Trace ⑫

Mistress Alyssa Sheridan (d) --- Jack

Key:
d = deceased
m = married
D = divorced
--- = illegitimate child

① Entangled
② A Rare Sensation
③ Society-Page Seduction
④ Just a Taste
⑤ Awaken the Senses
⑥ Estate Affair

⑦ Betrayed Birthright
⑧ Mistaken for a Mistress
⑨ Condition of Marriage
⑩ The Highest Bidder
⑪ Savor the Seduction
⑫ Name Your Price

# Prologue

*1968*

Spencer Ashton leaned back in his dark brown leather desk chair and allowed himself a smile. He'd come a long way from Nebraska in a very short time.

But not far enough.

His smile faded even as he turned in the chair to stare out the window at the palm trees waving in the wind. Palm trees—a symbol of California and a reminder of just how different his life was now in comparison to his old world. He caught the glimmer of his reflection in the sparkling glass and studied it. He knew his own attributes as well as he knew his bank balance. Paid to be honest—at least with yourself.

He was young, reasonably good-looking and ambitious. All traits that had served him well so far. Only three years with Lattimer Investment Banking and here he sat. In a corner office. He'd earned it. He'd toadied to John Lattimer, said all the right things, been all the right places and he'd *learned*. Learned enough to know that he'd never be satisfied working for someone else.

He wanted it all.

Wanted to put light-years between the man he was now and the man he'd been. If a brief flicker of guilt raced through his mind at the thought of the young wife and family he'd abandoned, he wiped it out fast. He hardly ever thought of Sally these days. Who had the time? He was a man on the fast track to success and wouldn't waste his energies by looking back.

Nodding slowly, thoughtfully, he decided then and there to *never* look back again. As of now, this moment, he had no past. He was starting over. A fresh slate. Nowhere to go but up.

The Lattimer Investment Banking business was a good step, he told himself. "But one day, it'll be Ashton Investments."

He could see it all so clearly. Himself, feared and admired by other lesser men. Employees jockeying for his good favor. Business rivals praying he wouldn't pull the rug out from beneath them. He would have a house twice as big as Lattimer's and he for damn sure wouldn't keep an employee as ambitious as himself around.

"Power," he murmured, smiling again as a late afternoon breeze tossed the long, lacy fronds of the trees right outside his office. "It all comes down to power. And what a man's willing to do to get it."

"Spencer?"

He stood up instantly at the sound of his boss's voice. Lattimer never knocked, damn it. Irritation scrambled through Spencer's system, but he quashed it with ruthless determination. He couldn't afford to piss off the old man. Not yet, anyway.

"John," Spencer said, smiling as though he wasn't imagining Lattimer out on a street corner with a tin cup and a handful of pencils. "Good to see you." Then he shifted his gaze to the young woman clinging to Lattimer's right arm.

Steering the petite blond woman farther into the office, John said, "I wanted you to meet Caroline, my daughter." He winked down at her. "My only child and the apple of my eye."

*Daughter?*

Why hadn't he known the old pirate had a kid?

Spencer's agile mind quickstepped. Pretty, in a nondescript, quiet way, Caroline Lattimer had green eyes, a nice figure and the polish and confidence of a woman raised with money. Obviously, her dear daddy doted on her, and Spencer, being a man who never failed to recognize opportunity when it stepped up and slugged him, gave her a slow smile.

She ducked her head, then looked up at him with, he was pleased to see, *interest.*

"Miss Lattimer," he said, taking her hand in both of his and feeling a quick jolt of pleasure at her nervous, indrawn breath, "I'm *very* pleased to meet you."

"Daddy's told me so much about you," she said, her voice quiet, cultured.

Shy, he thought and inwardly smiled. Though she was pretty enough and the daughter of a wealthy man, her own innate shyness had probably kept her from having too much experience with men.

Which only worked to his advantage.

Spencer kept her hand in his and stroked her skin with his thumb. And while she smiled up at him, he planned her seduction. His mind worked like a calculator as he figured out just how much time it would take to convince Lattimer's only child to fall in love with him.

Not long at all, if he played his cards right. And after that? Well, marrying into the boss's family was not exactly a *bad* idea.

After all, there was more than one way to get power.

And once he had it, he'd never let it go.

# One

*Present*

"**W**hat do you *mean* the bride's missing?" Megan Ashton stifled the instinct to lunge for her sister Paige's throat. No point in killing the messenger.

"I mean we can't find her," Paige said in a whispered rush, her hazel eyes darting from side to side. *"Anywhere."*

"Perfect." Megan plastered an unconcerned smile on her face and nodded absently at the handful of guests littering the small parlor. She couldn't afford to look worried.

Grabbing her sister's elbow, she steered Paige

across the room and out the right-side French doors leading to a wide stone veranda. When they were out of earshot, Megan reached up, took her headset off and clutched it in one tight fist. "Did you check the garden?"

Paige inhaled sharply, then blew the air out in a rush. "*Duh.* We checked everywhere. I even poked into every bathroom on the ground floor. She's nowhere, Megan. And I'm guessing she's not coming back."

"What do you mean?"

Paige sighed. "She left her wedding gown in the bride's room."

"Oh, God." Megan felt the first swirls of panic and fought them off as she would any other would-be attacker. As the event planner at Ashton Estates and Winery, she'd *never* had an event fail—and this would *not* be the first. All she had to do was think. Okay, think *fast.*

She glanced at her younger sister. Paige's light-brown layered hair ruffled in the breeze and worry glittered in her eyes. The Ashton family "genius," Paige had graduated college at nineteen, then she'd jumped right into business school at the University of Southern California, before leaving to come home and help out on the estate. Megan didn't know what she'd do without her.

Paige bit at her bottom lip and clenched her hands together at the waist of her simple black skirt. She shot an anxious glance toward the hall where wedding guests were still expecting the ceremony to take place in the next few minutes. "What're we supposed to do now?"

"What we *don't* do, is panic."

"Right. How do we do that?"

"Beats me," Megan muttered and lifted one hand to smooth back an errant lock of blond hair that had escaped the tidy ponytail at the back of her neck. Voices murmured behind her and a squawk came from the headset she was still clutching.

This was a nightmare.

Well, a potential nightmare.

Thoughts, ideas, plans raced through her mind, presented themselves and then were dismissed. None of them were good enough to pull this mess out of the fire. Blast it, what kind of woman ran away from her own wedding fifteen minutes before the ceremony?

And what in heaven's name was she supposed to tell the groom?

As if reading her mind, Paige shook her head. "I'm so not going to be the one to tell that groom his bride vamoosed."

Megan winced.

Simon Pearce, would-be groom and gazillionaire, was not going to take this news lightly. The man had arranged this wedding with all the care and diligence of an invasion. Having his plans quashed at the last minute was going to go over like a case of measles.

Megan reached up and rubbed a spot between her

eyes, but all she managed to do was massage a budding headache into a full-blown migraine.

She'd been dealing with Simon Pearce for more than a month now. He was gorgeous, irritating and rude. He snapped off orders and expected people to jump. In fact, until this morning, Megan had never once *seen* the blushing bride. Pearce had taken care of everything. He'd made all of the decisions concerning the wedding that wasn't going to be happening and right at the moment, Megan could almost understand why the bride scampered. She wasn't exactly looking forward to telling Mr. I-Know-Everything-Don't-Bother-Me-with-Details that he'd just been jilted.

"Oh ye gods," she murmured and lifted her face into the wind sweeping in from across the vineyard. The scent of the nearby ocean surrounded her and the chill of the March breeze cooled her heated cheeks. Unfortunately, it didn't do a thing for the knot in her stomach.

"That about covers it," Paige said and leaned back against the gray stone balustrade. Crossing her arms over her chest, she tipped her head to one side and asked, "So. What do you want me to do, boss?"

Megan nearly laughed. *Boss* indeed. Nobody told Paige what to do. Of course, that was probably an Ashton family trait, since Megan didn't take orders any better than her sister did.

And at that thought, memories of a conversation

she'd had with her father just two nights ago filled
her mind briefly before she shut them off. Another
man used to giving orders and expecting them to be
obeyed. But, she didn't have time right now to worry
about what Spencer Ashton was going to say when
she refused to go along with his latest plan.

At the moment, she had her own predicament to
pull out of the fire.

"This cannot be happening," she muttered and
started pacing, the sound of her heels clicking furiously against the polished river stones. "The food's
hot, the cake is gorgeous, the musicians have been
tuning up for a half hour." She threw her hands wide,
then let them slap down against her thighs. "There
are *reporters,* for heaven's sake, stationed right outside the hall. The minister's inside tapping his foot
and the groom is probably chewing on rocks. Why
would the stupid bride do this to me?"

"Um," Paige pointed out, "my guess is she wasn't
thinking about *you.*"

"Right." Megan inhaled slowly and exhaled the
same way. She tried a quick chant, but didn't have the
patience for that, so she jumped right back at her problem. "Okay, fine. We just have to do the best we can."

"And that is…?"

Megan pulled in another deep breath and held it
for a moment or two, just to steady herself. "You go
into the hall and mingle. Chat up the guests and keep
smiling, for pity's sake."

"Uh-huh," Paige said, pushing away from the stone railing. "Then what?"

"Then," Megan said, settling her phone's headset back into place, "*wait.* I'll talk to the groom, tell him what's going on and let him decide how he wants to handle it."

"Better you than me," Paige said.

Megan snorted. "Yeah. This must be why I make the big bucks, huh?"

Simon Pearce checked his gold wristwatch for the dozenth time in the last ten minutes. According to schedule, he should have entered the hall five minutes ago and even now be just about hitting the *I do* phase of the ceremony.

He tapped one finger against the glass face of the watch and tried to quell the licks of anger lapping at his insides. This delay would only foster more delays in the remainder of the day's schedule—and that was unacceptable.

"Want me to find out what's going on?"

Simon shook his head at his friend and assistant, Dave Healy. "No. Give it one more minute, then *I'll* ask some questions."

Dave shrugged and leaned one shoulder against the far wall. "It's your funeral."

"Wedding, you mean?"

Dave smiled. "All in the way you look at it."

"Right." Simon paced the confines of the small

antechamber off the main hall. Dave had never been in favor of Simon marrying Stephanie. Since Dave himself was happily married to his college sweetheart, he was under the impression that *love* should have something to do with a wedding. Well, Simon knew differently. Love only got in the way. Muddied the waters. Better to deal with a marriage as you would with any business merger.

He stalked to the wide bank of leaded windows overlooking the pool and gardens, and stared blankly out at the early spring day. Most of the trees were still bare-limbed and the rosebushes were just beginning to pop with buds. But there were a few splashes of deep rose and burnt orange from an assortment of fall and winter flowers lining the walkway leading to the pool house. He concentrated on those as his brain worked.

He thought of Stephanie Moreland, the woman he should have been marrying at that moment. They'd known each other for several months and when Simon had proposed only six weeks ago, she'd accepted with calm dignity. Exactly as he would have expected her to react.

She was just what he was looking for in a wife. Elegant, intelligent and wealthy enough in her own right that he needn't be worried she was after him for his money. Though there were no starry bursts of excitement when they were together, Simon was content enough. He needed a wife—specifically to help him in business. There were quite a few firms out there who were old-fashioned enough to think that an unmarried man was too unsettled to be trusted.

With Stephanie by his side, he could continue to grow Pearce Industries as planned.

"Which is *why*," he muttered, checking his watch yet again, "we need to get this wedding completed."

When the wide oak double doors behind him opened, Simon turned. The wedding planner stepped into the room, and his gaze pinned her in place.

Megan was a tall blond with cool green eyes and a limited store of patience. On more than one occasion over the last month or so of dealing with her, he'd seen her bite her lip to keep from arguing with one of his decisions. She seemed to be efficient, though, which was no doubt why the Ashtons kept her employed at their estate.

At the moment, however, she looked as though she'd prefer being anywhere but where she was.

One of his strengths in the world of business was reading the opposition's expressions. One look at the woman's troubled eyes and pinched mouth told him that he wasn't going to like whatever she had to say.

"Mr. Pearce."

He spoke up instantly and went right to the heart of the matter. "What seems to be the problem?"

She stepped into the room, closed the doors behind her and shot his assistant a quick look.

Simon did the same. Dave Healy shrugged and

slid his gaze back to the woman crossing the tiled floor with measured steps. Reading her hesitation correctly, Simon said, "You can speak freely in front of Mr. Healy."

"All right then," she said, swallowing hard and squaring her shoulders, "I'm sorry, Mr. Pearce, but your bride seems to have disappeared."

"Excuse me?" He bit the two words off.

But the cool blond wasn't affected by the simmering anger in his voice. She simply stared him down. "Ms. Moreland has left the estate."

"That's impossible."

"Apparently not."

Anger jittered inside him, but Simon put a lid on it, fast. Temper wasn't going to solve this problem. "Have you called her cell phone?"

"Yes," Megan said and once again shot an uneasy look at Dave. "She's not answering and her voice mail says that she'll be out of the country for the next few months."

Out of the country.

Quickly, Simon's brain raced back to his last conversation with his fiancée. He seemed to remember her saying something about moving to London for a while. But of course, he'd dismissed it out of hand, since he had too many business deals working at the moment to be that far away. It seemed though that Stephanie had decided to go without him.

Pushing the edges of his navy-blue jacket back, he

slid his hands into his slacks pockets and tried to think past the cold fury raging within. He'd selected his bride with care. He'd thought they were on the same wavelength. Marriage without messy emotions. A tidy merger of two families to the betterment of each of them.

Now he'd been jilted.

An old word, but appropriate.

Deep inside him, anger fluttered into life again.

Stephanie's leaving was a personal slap, certainly, but Simon wasn't hurt. Even now, he could admit that his bride's disappearance was more infuriating than devastating. He wasn't foolish enough to pretend, even to himself, that theirs had been a love match. Now, Simon considered the repercussions once word of this got out and didn't like the images his mind produced.

The scandal this would cause would set his merger with the Derry Foundation back weeks, if not months. The elder Derry was old school. He was only willing to deal with solid family men— and Simon didn't have the time to find another suitable wife.

Damn it.

This simply did *not* happen to Simon Pearce.

He never lost.

And he wasn't about to start now.

"I am sorry, Mr. Pearce," Megan was saying, and he shifted his gaze back to her. "If you'll tell me what you'd like me to say to your guests, I'll handle the announcements."

He studied her—not for the first time in the last month—and noticed just how lovely she was. Her blond hair was neatly drawn back from a heart-shaped face. Her wide green eyes were solemn now, but he'd seen them sparkling with laughter and dancing with indignation. She was intelligent, educated and coolly sophisticated. Over the last month, he'd noticed that she worked hard and had the ability to get things done. A trait he admired. She was even approximately the same size as Stephanie.

In short, she was perfect.

And frankly, the situation was just a little on the desperate side.

Studying her, he said, "Actually, Megan, I'd like to ask you a different sort of favor."

Puzzled, she glanced from him to Dave and back again.

Sensing her unease, Simon turned to his best friend and said, "Dave, give us a few minutes, will you?"

"Sure." The other man strode across the room, opened the doors, slipped through and then closed them again.

"What kind of favor did you have in mind?" Megan asked.

"It's one only *you* can help me with," Simon said, watching her eyes to more accurately gauge her response. "I'd like you to marry me."

# Two

At twenty-five, Megan had been in charge of event planning at her family's estate for three years. And in that time, she'd thought she'd seen it all. She'd held garden parties, Victorian teas, a baby shower for a senator's daughter, even a celebration for the oldest member of the local DAR chapter.

But this was the first time she'd been proposed to by a jilted groom.

Megan blinked, shook her head, then thunked the heel of her hand against her skull right above her left ear, as if trying to clear up a sudden case of deafness. "Are you crazy?"

"Not usually."

"Somehow, that's not really comforting."

He smiled, and she told herself to pay absolutely no attention to the sudden shift inside her. Weird re- action, and totally not the point. But she would dare any woman standing within three feet of the man to *not* feel the almost magnetic attraction he put out there.

Well over six feet, he had thick, wavy black hair that was stylishly cut to look as if it hadn't been styled. His eyes were the color of summer fog and his features looked as if they'd been carved from old oak by a loving sculptor. The man was a walking hor- mone-call to women.

"I'd like you to marry me," he said again as he checked his watch, then shifted his smoke gray eyes to her. "As quickly as possible."

She laughed shortly. *Marriage?* "You've got to be kidding."

That smoky gaze darkened as he fixed it on her and she felt the power of it right down to her bones.

"I never joke."

"Too bad," Megan muttered, thinking this had to be some sort of prank. "You'd be good at it."

This just wasn't happening, she thought, suddenly wishing his assistant would come back into the room. Because if Simon Pearce was actually serious, then he was a nut job.

"Look, Mr. Pearce—"

"Call me Simon."

"I don't think so. Mr. Pearce—"

"Megan," he interrupted her quickly. "I need a wife. I need to be married this afternoon."

"Why?"

"Why what?"

"Why the big rush to be married?"

"That's not really important."

"It is if you're asking me to be the bride."

He sighed, checked his watch again, then buttoned up his suit jacket. "Very well. Let's just say that a married man looks more 'settled' to some of the people I do business with."

"Are they Neanderthals?"

One corner of his mouth lifted and Megan caught herself hoping he'd smile again. Not a good sign. In the last month, she'd seen him impatient, harried and bored, but until a few minutes ago, she'd never seen him smile. Maybe he saved the most potent weapons for desperate situations.

"They're…*conservative,*" he explained.

"That's unfortunate—and weird, but I guess you know that and—"

"Megan," he interrupted again.

She had to bite down on a rush of temper. Seriously, did people let him get away with this all the time? "It's rude to interrupt."

"So it is," he acknowledged with a nod. "But I am in a hurry and I'd like you to hear my proposition before refusing out of hand."

Wouldn't hurt to let him talk, she told herself. Besides, he was taking this whole *the bride has left the building* news way better than she'd thought he would. "Okay, go ahead."

"Good. I need a wife," he said, "and you seem to fit the bill."

"By being female?"

"Certainly a step in the right direction."

She saw a flash in his eyes and felt the reaction hit her low and hard. "This is ridiculous," she pointed out.

From beyond the closed oak doors came the silky sounds of the string quartet hired to play for the guests. Outside, sunshine poured down on the Ashton family estate and slanted through the wide windows to lay in golden shadows on the tiled floor. And here in this room, a crazy man was making his pitch.

"Not really," he argued. "Arranged marriages have been around for centuries."

"Yes, and didn't they work out nicely? How many women, I wonder, ended up locked in towers or chained in dungeons...." Megan wished to heaven the man's assistant—or keeper—or whatever the heck he was, would come back inside.

He blew out an impatient breath. Ooh. Getting frustrated, was he?

"There's no dungeon at my house, I swear."

"Uh-huh."

"I'll give you whatever you want if you'll do me this favor."

"It's a little more than a favor," she pointed out. "Favors usually consist of walking your dog or feeding your fish or—"

"Money?" he coaxed. "How much would it take?"

"I'll ask my pimp," she snapped back, insulted.

He seemed to realize his mistake instantly and lifted both hands in apology. "Sorry. Sorry. What can I tempt you with, then?"

"Mr. Pearce..."

"I need to be married, Megan. There are reporters outside, television cameras. I can't avoid them, and the gossip surrounding a jilted bridegroom is something that would hurt my business." He scrubbed one hand across his face and suddenly looked a lot more...human than he had before. "The scandal would probably put my mother in a hospital."

Megan winced at the thought. Okay, it wasn't just business he was concerned about. That made her feel better—and worse. She couldn't marry a stranger to keep his mother out of the hospital, for heaven's sake.

Although, a small voice in the back of her mind taunted, her father wanted her to marry a veritable stranger for a lot more mercenary a reason.

Instantly, she snapped back to a scene in her father's study two nights before.

*"You're twenty-five now, Megan," he said, studying her as he would a horse he was considering buying.*

*Megan half expected him to inspect her teeth, but*

*kept her thoughts to herself, since Spencer Ashton was never interested in anyone's opinion but his own.*

*"And it's time you married."*

*She scrambled for something to say, but couldn't come up with anything.* Married? *She'd hardly dated in over a year—not since her last boyfriend had accepted a tidy buyout from her father.*

*"And," Spencer went on and she listened, knowing that forewarned was forearmed, "since your taste in men is abysmal, I've taken the liberty of finding you a suitable husband."*

*"Excuse me?"*

*"Husband, Megan. I'm sure you know the word."*

*"Yes, and I appreciate it, Father, but—"*

*"William Jackson," Spencer said and leaned back in his oversize, dark maroon leather chair. He braced his elbows on the armrests and studied her over his steepled fingers. "Son of* Senator *Jackson."*

*"Willie?" Horrified, she took a step toward the desk, amazed that her knees were still holding her upright. "You want me to marry Willie Jackson?"*

*"Senator Jackson has agreed," he said quietly, "that once our children are married, he will speed up the passage of a certain bill that will go a long way toward solidifying my enterprises here on the Coast."*

*Ah... There it was. This wasn't about Megan, not that she'd really considered it was. This was about helping Spencer's business. And really? Didn't every conversation eventually wander back to the most important thing in his life? Ashton Industries?*

"So basically," Megan said before she could think better of it, "you get Willie a wife and the senator gives you California."

Spencer frowned tightly and Megan felt the very familiar sensation of a cold stone dropping to the pit of her stomach. She'd done it again. It never failed. She'd been trying most of her life to win her father's approval, but no matter what, she always seemed to come up short.

But Willie Jackson?

"You could do worse. William is a fine young man from a good family."

Keep quiet, *her brain insisted, but her tongue just didn't get the message in time.*

"He's an idiot," Megan blurted. "A sweetheart, but an idiot."

"That'll be enough," Spencer muttered and sat up straight, resting his forearms atop his meticulously neat desk. "William Jackson is the man for you."

"Father," Megan argued, "the man goes to sci-fi conventions with his dog."

Spencer winced.

"In matching costumes," she added.

"You'll help him to mature."

"I won't do it." *Good heavens, had she really said that? Even as the words rushed from her mouth, Megan actually* saw *them, dancing in the air before her eyes. Like colorful splashes on a blackboard, they stood out in the room, refusing to be overlooked.*

*Her stomach spasmed and she felt the way she had as a child, when she was waiting for a punishment she knew was coming. She clenched her hands at her sides and lifted her chin in spite of the dread swamping her. She had to draw a line somewhere, didn't she? She had to be a grown-up at some point. Had to stand up to the man who'd been both hero and dragon in her life. She had to speak up for herself or end up married to Willie and sewing sequins onto his dog's cape.*

*"I don't believe I heard you correctly."*

*"Yes you did, Father. I'm not going to marry Willie."*

*His features darkened, color rising up from his throat like an incoming tide. His eyes flashed and his mouth thinned into a grim slash of disapproval.*

*And still, Megan stood her ground.*

*Her knees were wobbly, but she stood it.*

*"We'll discuss this when you're more rational."*

*"I'm perfectly rational."*

*"No, you are not. What you are," he said, "is dismissed." He didn't look at her again. Instead, he opened a drawer, pulled out a manila folder, picked up a fountain pen and began to work—as if she were already gone. As if everything were settled. As if she'd already agreed to the marriage.*

*Which was, of course, exactly the way he saw it.*

And Megan thought now, as she resurfaced from the memory, her father was just relentless enough to eventually wear her down. Spencer Ashton would never give up. Unless she was already married...

"Look at this like a business proposition," Simon was saying.

"Business."

He perked up, his gray eyes sparkling with anticipation as he realized she was beginning to waver. "I'll give you anything you want," he said.

Was craziness contagious? she wondered. Was she seriously considering agreeing to marry Simon Pearce? Okay, yes. Because here, she could call the shots. And, it would give her the added benefit of being able to face her father and explain that it was impossible for her to marry Willie.

Besides, how bad could it be?

Simon was gorgeous, rich and—okay, crazy. But mental stability wasn't that big a deal, right? Of course, there was crazy and then there was *Willie* crazy.

"Do you have a dog?" she blurted.

"Huh?" His brows drew together. "No."

"Okay," she said on a sigh of relief, "that's good."

"If you say so," he murmured, giving her a look that said plainly he had a few concerns about *her* stability.

"I have a few conditions," Megan said.

He nodded. "I'm listening."

Oh God, she was really going to do this. Her stomach swirled and her hands went damp. But she started speaking quickly, not giving herself a chance to second-guess this nutso decision. "We have to stay married for one full year."

"A year?"

"Yes." That way, she'd have enough time to find a woman for Willie. Impossible though that seemed at the moment, she firmly believed in the old adage that there was *someone for everyone.*

He thought about it for a long moment, then nodded. "Agreed."

Okay, that was easy. *"And,"* she added, "no one can know that I'm just a last-minute replacement bride." She started pacing, feeding the nervous energy pounding through her system. "I don't care how you explain it—say we were swept away or that it was love at first sight—whatever." She stopped, turned around and stared at him, her gaze locking with his. "I won't have your friends and family thinking I'm just the emergency wife."

"Love at first sight?" he mused, that half smile tugging at his lips again.

"It could happen."

"If you say so." Folding his arms over his chest, he tipped his head to one side and asked, "Is that it? No more conditions?"

"One more." If she was going to do this, then she was going to do it right. She wouldn't have people whispering or feeling sorry for her or being embarrassed by a "husband" who was still dating. "I expect you to be faithful for the duration. No cheating whatsoever."

His eyes narrowed to match hers. "I don't cheat," he said tightly. "And I'll expect the same from you."

Megan stared into his eyes for a long minute and was reassured by his steady gaze. She nodded, relieved on that score anyway. "Agreed."

"Good. Any more conditions?"

"No, I think that does it."

Simon was stunned. He'd expected her to ask for money. *Lots* of it. And frankly, he'd have been more than happy to pay. But she'd surprised him and that didn't happen often. Intrigued, he studied the woman he was about to marry and wondered how many other surprises she had in store for him.

"So it's a deal?" she asked, walking closer and holding out her right hand.

He looked down at her slim white palm, then lifted his gaze to hers. "Not quite yet. I've a condition of my own."

"Which is?"

"If we're going to stay married for a year," he said, "and neither one of us will be…'dating' anyone else, then it will be a *real* marriage."

"Meaning?" She swallowed. Hard.

"I think you know what I mean," he said, then reached out and took her hand in both of his. Her skin was smooth, soft and icy with nerves. "When I make a deal, I don't cheat—"

"Neither do I," she said quickly.

"Good. But I'm not going to live a year without sex, either."

"Um…" She tried to slip her hand from his, but he only held on tighter. Megan had lived the last year without sex and she hadn't exactly withered up and died—but she had a feeling a man like Simon Pearce wasn't used to going without female company for longer than a few days at a stretch. And, if she were going to be honest here, at least inwardly, she could admit that being celibate wasn't all it was cracked up to be.

Scowling then, she tipped her chin up and met his gaze squarely. "I guess that's reasonable. Okay then, shall we say, once a month?"

He laughed. "Twice a day."

Her eyebrows shot straight up. "What're you, a rabbit?"

He smiled and told himself that a year with this woman was going to be way more interesting than marriage to Stephanie would have been. Never once in the several months he'd known her had Stephanie surprised him. Or made him want to laugh. Megan, though, was a different story altogether. Certainly he'd known she'd never go for sex twice a day. But a smart negotiator started high.

"You have a problem with twice a day, then?"

She nodded. "You could say so. How about once every three weeks?"

He shook his head and rubbed his thumb across the back of her hand. "Once a day."

She blew out a breath and a stray lock of blond hair ruffled slightly, then drooped down to lie alongside her cheek. Narrowing her eyes at him, she offered, "Once every two weeks."

"Every other day."

She scowled at him. "You know, I could probably think better if you'd let go of my hand."

"I like your hand."

"You're an interesting man, Mr. Pearce."

"Thank you. And it's *Simon*."

"Fine. Simon. Once a week."

He hadn't enjoyed a negotiation so much in years. He could see the wheels in her brain working and told himself that this emergency marriage might be more entertaining than he had a right to expect. "Three times a week."

"Two."

"Done."

"Oh, boy." She cleared her throat, nodded jerkily, then snatched her hand free of his grasp.

He didn't want to think about why his fingertips suddenly itched to touch her again. About why his hand felt *empty* without hers in it.

"One more thing," she said and had his attention again.

"Which is…?"

She reached up and tucked that stray lock of hair behind her right ear, and for the first time, Simon noticed the flash of small diamond-stud earrings.

"The, uh, *wedding night,*" she said, her voice starting out soft and picking up strength as she continued. "You're not expecting it to start tonight, right?"

The purely male part of him wanted exactly that. He wanted to feel her skin beneath his hands. He wanted to peel her out of her very attractive but sensible black skirt and white silk blouse. Desire boiled within, sudden and nearly overwhelming and it was that realization more than anything that had him reassuring her. He wasn't a man to be led by his hormones.

"Why don't we take a little time to get to know each other?"

She smiled and he read mischief in her eyes as she asked, "Say, six months?"

"Is this going to be another negotiation?" he asked. "Because if it is, you're starting high."

"I learn fast."

He nodded, amused in spite of himself. "How about a week?"

She hesitated.

"*One* week," he repeated.

She tipped her head up to meet his gaze directly. She thought about it for a long minute, then slowly nodded. "One week."

Her grass-green eyes glittered and the pulse at the base of her throat pounded. When she licked dry lips and swallowed hard, Simon drew in a long, deep breath to steady himself. Why hadn't he paid closer attention to her over the last month? How had he *not* noticed those eyes? That mouth?

To disguise the unexpected thoughts racing through his mind, Simon checked his watch one more time. "You should go put your wedding gown on. I'll tell the minister we'll be ready in five minutes."

She shook her head sadly. "You seriously have a clock fixation, don't you?"

"Just one of my many attributes."

"Or curses."

He smiled. He could afford to now. He'd turned a near disaster into a triumph. "Megan, you'll be able to spend the next year learning my every quirk. But right now…"

"Right. Get dressed. Get married." She turned for the door, her heels clicking noisily against the tiles. When she reached the door, she grabbed the knob and looked back over her shoulder at him. "Sure hope you know what you're getting us into."

Then she was gone and Simon could only tell himself that *of course* he knew what he was doing.

He *always* knew.

# Three

Late-morning sunlight darted through the floor-to-ceiling windows lining the great hall. The dark crimson silk draperies were open wide and the spotless window glass sparkled like diamonds in the light.

Only a handful of guests were seated in the deeply cushioned white chairs staggered on both sides of a narrow aisle. At the head of that aisle, a minister stood, bible open on his palms. Beside him, Simon waited, tall and gorgeous, his gaze locked on Megan.

As she moved slowly down the aisle, following her sister Paige, still wearing her pale-yellow blouse and simple black skirt, Megan had the opportunity to question her own sanity. She was wearing another woman's wedding dress, and though it was beautiful, it wasn't one she'd have chosen for herself. Ivory lace covered her arms and chest, and the silk beneath if felt cool against her skin. The skirt of the dress was wide, brushing against the rungs of the chairs as she passed and the sound it made was like anxious whispers. She was about to marry another woman's fiancé, in front of witnesses she didn't know. And in about a week, she'd be sharing her bed with a man who would be both a stranger and her husband.

Her head was spinning, so she stopped thinking.

Paige, only a step or two ahead of her on the aisle, was the only member of Megan's family present—not exactly how she'd imagined her wedding day, by any means. She could still hear Paige's arguments and every one of them had been logical and rational.

Yet none of them had been strong enough to dissuade her. If there was one thing Megan could admit about herself, it was that once her mind was made up, that decision was set in concrete. Besides, if she had a choice between Simon Pearce and Willie the Weird, she'd pick Simon anytime.

Paige paused at the head of the aisle and Megan knew without actually having to see it that her younger sister was giving Simon a *hurt-my-sister-and-die* look. And she smiled to herself, grateful as always to know that Paige was on her side. No matter what.

The former bride's family and attendants had left.

Simon had spoken to the minister and now everyone here—with the exception of the bride—was relaxed and ready. Heck, by pulling a few strings, Simon had even managed to procure an emergency marriage license. In his own way, Simon was every bit as powerful as Spencer Ashton.

Megan shivered at the thought.

Then she stepped up beside Simon, took a deep breath and felt his fingers close around her right hand. Warm, she thought. Warm and strong and somehow...comforting.

The minister started talking and, truth to tell, she wasn't listening. She was having what felt like an out-of-body experience. She couldn't be sure of course, since it had never happened before, but what else could explain the light-headedness? The ringing in her ears? The blurry swim to her vision?

"I do," Simon said, his deep voice reverberating through the room before dancing along her spine, sending her nerve endings into a frantic skip.

*Oh, boy.*

Her turn.

Megan focused her gaze on the minister and noted the beads of sweat on his forehead and idly wondered if he was as nervous as she was. He seemed nice enough. She'd spoken to him about last-minute details only an hour ago. Of course then, neither one of them had known *she* would be the bride.

"I, Megan Ashton," she said, repeating the ancient words as the reverend led her carefully through her vows.

Beside her, Simon stiffened. *Ashton?* As in Ashton Estates? Ashton Winery? Ashton, dozens of other enterprises?

He wondered why she hadn't told him. Then reminded himself that he'd been working with the woman for the last month or more and had never inquired of her last name. Hadn't seemed important. She'd simply been Megan, the event planner.

He stared down at the woman swearing to be faithful to him and only to him and he at least understood why he hadn't been able to coax her into this wedding with the promise of *money.*

And while his thoughts raced, he realized that this emergency marriage was going to be complicated. He'd long been a favorite of the paparazzi that made their living stalking celebrities. But Simon Pearce marrying one of the Ashton heirs would have those notorious photographers—not to mention reporters—slavering like wild dogs. The Ashton family was as well-known as his own and the media would have a field day if they got wind that this marriage was anything but the real deal.

"You may kiss the bride."

Simon's thoughts dissolved at the words and he turned to face Megan. All around them, people watched but all he could see were her eyes. Brilliant, grass-green eyes. Sparkling with humor, wariness and just a touch of regret.

"Second thoughts?" he whispered, lifting one hand to smooth another stray lock of hair behind her ear.

One corner of her mouth quirked. When she spoke, her voice was as hushed as his. "Oh, yeah. Second thoughts and thirds and fourths and—"

He silenced her the best way he knew how. Bending his head, he covered her mouth with his, cutting her off mid-sentence. A flash of something unexpected leaped through him and caught Simon completely off guard.

Lifting his head again, he stared at her as if seeing her for the first time. She looked as surprised as he felt. There was heat here. Something he hadn't felt in—well, ever. And he wasn't entirely sure that was a good thing.

This was a marriage of convenience—in the most literal terms. Thinking it was anything else would only cause more problems.

And yet...

Unable to deny himself, Simon bent to kiss her again and instantly felt that jolt of lightning-like sensation shoot through him. Her mouth surrendered to his.

She leaned into him, tipping her head back farther as she lifted onto her toes to meet his kiss.

Desire pulsed through him with the rattle and roar of thunder. Reaction shuddered through Megan, too, and her response fed his own.

He forgot where they were.

Forgot they were strangers.

And lost himself in the taste of her.

Pressing her close to his body, he held her tightly, firmly, until he could feel her every curve. The delicate lace of her gown scraped against his fingertips. Her scent, a faint floral blend, filled his head. His tongue swept into her mouth as he fed the urge within him clamoring for more. She was warm and sweet and open and he dived into her, groaning, giving himself up to the sensations coursing through him.

She clung to him, giving as much as she took. Her breath brushed his cheek, her hands slid up his back and when she sighed into his mouth, Simon felt the slam of it as he would have a punch to the middle.

Applause.

Laughter.

These sounds and more finally worked their way past the fog of passion clouding Simon's mind. Slowly, reluctantly, he ended the kiss and looked down at her. Her pale skin was suffused with color, her mouth looked full and puffy, her eyes dazzling in the sunlight. He wanted her more than he'd ever wanted anything in his life.

And because the urge to take her had him by the throat, Simon gritted his teeth and took a deliberate step back from her—distancing himself not only from his new bride, but from the very real threat of losing his self-control. Something he'd never done before.

Something he *never* allowed to happen.

Forcing a smile, he took her hand and turned to face the guests already crowding up the aisle to congratulate them.

"Everything's running smoothly, so stop worrying—at least about the reception," Paige said.

"It just feels strange to not be running around checking on everyone," Megan told her and smoothed one hand down the front of her secondhand wedding gown.

"Uh-huh." Paige looked at her with wide eyes and shook her head. "It's strange to you to not be running the show, but *not* strange to be married to a man you don't know?"

"Okay," Megan admitted, letting her gaze slide over the small crowd until it landed on *her husband*. "That's strange, too."

"I can't believe you did this."

"Yes, well, me neither," Megan said and told herself she was imagining the heat of Simon's gaze. "But better him than poor Willie."

"Father never would have made you go through with that," Paige insisted.

Megan shifted her younger sister a sharp look. "Have you *met* our father?"

"Okay, maybe he would." Paige pushed her hair back out of her eyes, covered the mouthpiece of the headset she wore with one hand and whispered, "But what do you think he's going to say when he finds out what you did?"

Oh, Megan didn't want to think about that. She really didn't. Already, her stomach was churning in anticipation of the showdown that was looming in her near future. Her father would be furious. But, even he couldn't make her marry someone else when she was already married.

Laying one hand flat against her stomach, Megan breathed deeply, an old trick she'd been practicing for years. Deep, slow, even breaths were usually enough to curb the roiling nausea that confrontations with her father were sure to cause.

"Yes," Paige said, speaking now into the headset. "I'll be right there."

"What is it?" Megan asked. "What's wrong?"

"Nothing I can't handle," Paige murmured and gave her sister's hand a pat. "Just a minor crisis in the kitchen."

"If it's Jean complaining about the caterer again, tell him I said that he has to—"

"You're the bride today, remember?" Paige asked, already stalking toward the back of the hall and the kitchens beyond. "I'll handle it."

Megan nodded and fought the urge to run and take care of the problems herself. Since being put in charge of the events planning at the estate, she'd made a real name for herself. She worked hard, took care of every detail and had never had an event fail.

"Thinking of skipping out on me?" Simon's deep voice came from right behind her. Startled, Megan jumped and turned to face him.

"Sneak up on people often?"

"Didn't sneak. Walked."

"Well, walk louder," she suggested and tried to look past him at his guests, on the other side of the hall.

"Time for some pictures," he said and took her elbow in a firm grip.

"Oh, Simon, I don't think we—"

"A *real* marriage," he whispered, dipping his head so that his breath dusted her ear. "Remember?"

"Right."

First, the happy couple stepped out into the sunlight for the benefit of the media gathered outside the reception hall. Cameras clicked, reporters shouted questions and through it all, Simon kept a proud smile on his face and one arm around Megan's shoulders—just in case she got cold feet and made a run for it.

But she didn't. To give her her due, she stood her ground, lifted her chin and smiled beautifully for the media. He doubted Stephanie could have handled the situation as smoothly.

Once the news frenzy was over, they stepped back inside to be surrounded by the small cluster of guests. More cameras flashed while people smiled and offered congratulations. Simon kept his arm around her shoulders and held her close, playing the part of a doting groom to perfection. Megan chatted, smiled and posed for pictures until her cheeks hurt from smiling. She accepted champagne from a server and took a long gulp, hoping it would soothe her dry throat and scattered emotions.

Simon's mother, a small, elegant-looking woman with short, stylishly cut silver hair, wearing a pale-blue designer suit, dabbed at teary eyes and gave Megan a warm hug. "My dear," she muttered, "you look lovely."

"Thank you, Mrs. Pearce."

"Please," the woman said, "call me Phoebe. I just know that you and I are going to be good friends."

Oh, Megan felt awful. Phoebe was being so nice and Megan was lying. To her. To everyone there.

Desperately, she tried to think of *something* to say even while wondering why Simon hadn't explained any of this to his own mother, at least.

"Phoebe, I'm so sorry I didn't get to meet you before, but this was all very sudden and—"

"Never mind, honey," Phoebe interrupted as smoothly as her son made a habit of doing and Megan knew immediately where he'd picked up the trait. "I never cared for Stephanie, you know. Cold eyes. But you—" she stopped, reached up and cupped Megan's cheek. "You have good eyes. And a lovely smile. I know you'll make my son very happy."

*Oh man.*

Could guilt actually *kill* a person?

The next couple of hours passed in a blur. Dinner and cake were served, and never once did anyone mention the fact that the bride had been exchanged at the last minute. The handful of people attending the ceremony were there for Simon and apparently, Megan thought, Simon Pearce wielded even more power than her father. Enough so that a change of bride didn't merit the flicker of an eyelash.

By the time the party was over and Megan was back in the bride's room changing into her own clothes, she felt as though it had all been a strange sort of stage play. And now that the play was over, the lead actress could go back to her everyday job.

Until Simon opened the door.

"Hey!" She snatched up the wedding dress she'd just peeled off and held it to her chest like a Victorian maiden. "Do you mind?"

"Not at all," he said, one corner of his mouth lifting as he stepped into the small antechamber and closed the door behind him.

Megan blew out a breath and glared at him.

It didn't faze him.

"I'd like a little privacy," she said when it became clear he wasn't going anywhere.

"We're married now, Megan," he retorted and sat down on an armchair near the door.

"We don't even know each other," she reminded

him and sidestepped to the adjoining bathroom, still clutching the dress in front of her.

"We have to start somewhere."

"Not while I'm undressed."

"Fine. I'll close my eyes."

She opened the bathroom door, stepped behind it and peeked around the corner at him. "I don't trust you."

"Hardly the start of a happy marriage," he said, head tipped back, eyes closed.

Working quickly, Megan dropped the wedding gown and reached around behind her for her skirt and blouse. Pulling her clothes on, she talked while she moved. "This isn't your ordinary marriage though, is it?"

"It could be," he said.

She sneaked another peek at him. Eyes still closed. That was something, she supposed, and hurriedly buttoned up her blouse, then tucked the hem beneath the waistband of her skirt.

"Your mother *likes* me," she said.

"You say that like it's a bad thing."

"It is. We're lying to her. And I don't like it."

"I'll explain everything to my mother."

"Good. She seems nice." Megan bent down, grabbed up one of her black three-inch heels and slipped it on, then did the same with the other.

Finally dressed and feeling just a little more in control of the situation, she stepped out from behind the open bathroom door and said, "It's okay, you can open your eyes now."

He did, then stood up and walked across the room to stand in front of her. "Why didn't you tell me you were an Ashton?"

She cocked her head to one side and stared up at him. "I worked with you for a month, Simon. It wasn't a secret."

"But you never said."

"You never asked."

"True," he admitted, then unbuttoned his suit jacket, brushed the edges of the jacket back and jammed his hands into his pockets. "I should have. As it is, you being an Ashton is going to make this more…complicated."

"How?"

Late-afternoon sunlight shone through the windows overlooking the gardens and the pool beyond. The scent of roses filled the air, riding on a soft breeze that swept through the partially opened window.

"The newspapers will be more interested than ever in our marriage. You must see that."

She hadn't thought of it, but she supposed he was right. Heaven knew the media was always hounding her father about one thing or another. But growing up in the public eye, she tended to forget about it. Now though, she was beginning to see that being the daughter of a powerful man and the wife of another could make her more interesting to photographers and reporters.

"It's just for a year," she reminded him.

"Yes, but now it's more important than ever that we present the facade of a *real* marriage." He took two steps away, stared out the window, then shifted her a look. "The honeymoon in Fiji is a good start of course." He checked his watch and nodded to himself as if making a mental note. "We'll just have time for you to pack—don't worry about bringing a lot, we'll make a quick stop in Paris so you can shop."

An offer that would have had most women quivering in anticipation. But Megan was not most women.

*"Fiji?"* She shook her head. "Sorry, I can't."

"What do you mean, you can't?" he snapped and turned to face her. "You agreed to play this part, Megan."

"The part of a marriage, yes. The honeymoon thing? No thanks. I have a job."

He laughed shortly. "A job? You work for your family."

Megan stiffened. Happened every time someone assumed that she was a spoiled little rich girl just amusing herself by throwing parties.

"My job's important to me. And I'm good at it," she said tightly. "And in the next two weeks, I have two weddings and a sixteenth-birthday party here on the estate. I can't leave. And I wouldn't even if I could."

"Really?" he asked, his eyes narrowing. "And why's that?"

"Because, Simon," she said, walking toward him and not stopping until she was close enough to jab him in the chest with her index finger, "I may be the surprise exchange bride, and I may get married wearing someone else's idea of a gown and I even may be forced to wear a ring—" she waved her hand in his face for emphasis "—chosen for someone else, but I'll be damned if I'm going on another woman's honeymoon."

Simon frowned at her. "What's wrong with the ring?"

He'd missed the whole point. Not surprising though, Megan thought as she drew her head back and looked at him in stunned stupefaction. "It's not *mine*," she said flatly and looked down at the gaudy, wide gold band, boasting a too-big diamond surrounded by emeralds.

She'd never have chosen anything like it and the fact that she was stuck with it was only going to be a constant reminder that her marriage *wasn't* real. That she'd married a stranger. That she'd picked up another woman's castoff and had made it hers.

"You don't like diamonds?"

He sounded so surprised, she almost laughed. "Every woman likes diamonds," she replied. "But I don't like yellow gold and I don't like gigantic rings that will get caught on everything and I don't like emeralds."

He frowned thoughtfully. "I could—"

"Never mind," she said and felt good interrupting him for a change. "It doesn't matter. I said I'd do this and I will. But I'm not going to pretend to go on a honeymoon to Fiji, of all places, with a man I don't know."

Silence thundered around them for a long minute when she stopped speaking, until finally Simon said, "It's been a long time since anyone's had the nerve to argue with me like that."

Megan laughed shortly and headed for the door. "Welcome to your new world."

"Where are you going?" he demanded.

"Back to work," she said tightly. "I've got preparations to finalize for next week's wedding."

When she walked out, Simon was left alone, the only sound to be heard, the steady click of her heels as she left him.

# Four

"**Y**ou're really certifiable, aren't you?" Paige leaned against the wall in Megan's office, feet crossed at the ankles, arms folded over her chest. "Not only do you marry strangers, but now, you're refusing a honeymoon in Fiji?"

Megan spared her sister a quick glance, then looked back at her computer screen. Two hours since the wedding and none of it felt real. She still couldn't believe she'd actually done it. But the gaudy ring on her left hand was proof enough to remind her.

She'd tried not to think about what she'd signed up for. Maybe Simon had caught her in a weak moment. Maybe if she'd taken her time and thought about it, she wouldn't have agreed. But, if she hadn't, then she'd still be dealing with the problem of her father and Willie-the-would-be-groom.

Which was enough to make her shudder.

"I've got work here, Paige. I can't just take off for two weeks."

"Right. Because no one else but you is qualified to make some phone calls and keep caterers in line."

Megan sighed and leaned back in her chair. Her office was just behind the main reception hall on the first floor of the estate. Here in this room, she'd created her own little world. The walls were a soft rose, complementing the rough brick of the fireplace on one wall. Muted impressionist paintings lined the other walls and the furniture was feminine without being overdone. The room was warm, welcoming, and as unlike the rest of the Ashton family showplace as she could make it.

Through a connecting door that led into the catering kitchen, she could hear the low rumble of voices and the occasional rattle of dishes. Through the bay windows overlooking the broad expanse of lawn at the front of the house, she had a view of the wide circular driveway with the oversize reflecting pool dead center.

And at the moment, her new husband was standing beside that pool, cell phone clapped to one ear.

Paige strolled toward the front windows, then glanced back at her sister. Wiggling her eyebrows, she urged, "*Look* at him, Megan. The man's gorgeous. Who *wouldn't* want to get him off onto an island and out of that oh-so-elegantly tailored suit?"

"Me, that's who." Megan blew out a breath then stood up and walked around her desk. Crossing the soft oriental carpet stretched out across a cold marble floor, she stopped alongside her sister and watched the man she'd married. "Okay, fine. He's easy to look at."

"Easy? Oh, he's better than that."

"Yeah. He really is." And that kiss, Megan thought, remembering the first touch of his mouth on hers. She hadn't expected to feel so much *everything*. It had been like standing in the middle of a power plant when there was a system overload. Sparks, lights, electrical charges jumping through her body. "But it doesn't matter."

Paige reached out and touched her hand to Megan's forehead. "Nope. No fever."

"Funny." Megan pushed her sister's hand aside. Watching as Simon reached up and pushed one hand through his wind-tousled hair, she swallowed hard and then told herself to get a grip. She didn't have anything to worry about. They'd already agreed that there wouldn't be any sex for a week.

And why, she thought, was she suddenly regretting that little agreement? Because Paige was right, she told herself. She *was* certifiable.

"Well," Paige said with a shake of her head, "I still say you should have gone to Fiji."

"I can't."

"Okay, I get it," her sister said. "But you should at least leave *here* before Father gets home. Unless you want your wedding day and the day of your death to be remembered with one fond anniversary."

"Oh man…" There'd been so much going on, so much to think about, she'd completely forgotten about Spencer Ashton. She hadn't wanted to consider her father at all. Because once she did, she'd have to face up to the task of telling him that she'd shattered his dreams regarding Senator Jackson.

And that scene wouldn't be a pretty one.

Megan's stomach twisted at the thought. All her life, she'd tried to please Spencer. She'd tried to be the kind of daughter he wanted. The kind of Ashton heir he expected. As a girl, she used to dream of having him *really* look at her one day and say, *I'm proud of you, Megan.*

Though she hated to admit it, even to herself, there was still a piece of that little girl inside her. Still waiting for Daddy's approval. It didn't seem to matter that she'd grown up. That she'd accepted long ago that Spencer Ashton would never be the kind of father she'd once dreamed of.

"And that's not even taking Mother into account," Paige muttered.

"Oh, this just gets better and better," Megan said. Why hadn't she thought this through? Now she was stuck having to tell both her parents that she was married and to try to explain why neither of them had been present. Good times.

"So what're you going to do?"

Megan shot her sister a quick look, then headed back toward her desk. Snatching her purse out of the bottom drawer, she slammed the drawer shut again and stood up. "I'm going to take your advice and get out of here. Fast."

Simon Pearce was not a man to be brushed off.

So he for damn sure wasn't going to be ignored by his new wife.

*Wife.*

He was married to one of the Ashtons. And he wondered if that meant he'd have to be civil to Spencer. That went against the grain. Spencer Ashton had the reputation of a hungry barracuda, and the scruples of a con man bilking a church lady out of her life savings.

Late-afternoon sunlight sparkled on the surface of the reflecting pool and Simon squinted against the glare. A warm breeze ruffled the still water and brushed past him, carrying the nearly cloying scent of roses from the well-manicured garden.

He tightened his grip on the cell phone in his hand and tried to concentrate on what Dave Healy was saying. But it wasn't easy.

"Simon, if you're not headed to Fiji as planned, then why can't you take the meeting with the Franklin company?"

Damn it, he'd worked for the last four weeks to clear his schedule long enough to allow a honeymoon. And now that he had the time, he wasn't at all sure he wanted to give it up. "Because whether or not we leave town together, Megan and I have to at least give the *impression* of being happy newlyweds."

"You really think this is a good idea?"

Actually, Simon had been wondering that himself, from the moment Megan announced her full name to the minister. An Ashton, for God's sake. What were the odds of his *accidentally* marrying a woman whose family was more well-known than his own?

He reached up and scraped one hand across his face. The media were going to be all over them for at least the next few weeks. Hell, there'd probably be paparazzi hiding in his oak trees, with telephoto lenses aimed at his house.

Simon had already seen the avaricious glitter in the eyes of the reporters. He'd smoothly explained away the fact that Megan's parents hadn't attended her wedding by saying that it had been a spur of the moment thing—then tried to gloss over the fact that his *own* mother had been there. This was going to get complicated. The very least he needed was a few days to talk to Megan. To make their plans. To learn how to face the world as a united front. Or the jig would be up almost before it began.

"It's the *only* idea," Simon said. "Besides, it's done and over with now. Megan and I are married and we'll handle whatever comes next."

Dave gave a long-suffering sigh and Simon almost smiled. "Fine. I'll handle Franklin. Good luck with the little woman."

"Right." Simon snapped the cell phone closed and half turned to look at the ostentatious facade of the Ashton estate.

Cream-colored stone seemed to glow in the late afternoon light. The mansion squatted at the top of a hill, giving its residents a beautiful view of the vineyards below. Window glass winked at him as the sun slanted across the front of the house and Simon scowled at the place. It looked like one of those mansions built in the last century by robber barons with more money than taste.

He'd heard people say that, when the house was owned by the Lattimer family, it had been smaller, yet elegant. But once Spencer Ashton took over, he'd "improved" it. He'd added two massive wings, tacked on conical towers at the end of each wing and, in general, taken a nice little country house and transformed it into a palace.

And it felt as warm as its cool marble floors.

Slipping his cell phone into his jacket pocket, Simon started across the crushed gravel drive, headed for the front doors. Past time to retrieve his wife and get started on their faux marriage.

* * *

"What're you supposed to pack for your marriage?" Megan muttered, throwing the doors to her walk-in closet wide. Okay, fine, she'd be sending for *all* of her things if she was going to be married for a year. But for right now, she needed to throw a few things together.

The question was, what?

Blindly, she stalked into the closet, swept an armful of clothing off the rack and walked back to the queen-size bed where her suitcase lay open and waiting. She'd been packing for herself for years, despite her mother always insisting that it was the maid's job to do those little chores. Megan liked knowing what she'd have and what she wouldn't. No point in being surprised.

So as she worked quickly, efficiently, her mind was already racing ahead to the other things she'd need. Makeup, hairbrushes, did her new husband have a blow dryer? She'd better take hers.

In fact, she was so busy with the task at hand, she didn't hear her mother enter the room.

"Would you care to explain?"

Megan's hands stilled and she winced a little before looking up to see Lilah Jensen Ashton standing at the foot of the bed.

At forty-nine, Megan's mother was still a beauty. Her chin-length red hair, kept looking natural by frequent trips to her favorite salon, was elegantly casual as always. Her cream-colored designer pants set was jazzed up by the dark-crimson silk blouse she wore beneath her jacket. Gold gleamed dully at her ears and her wrists. Thanks to a diet of coffee and salads, Lilah's figure was as trim as it had been when she'd first gone to work as Spencer Ashton's secretary. Her blue eyes were sharp and rarely missed much.

"Hello, Mother." Megan straightened up and prepared herself. Confrontations with her mother had been few and far between over the years. Though Megan loved her mother, she also knew that Lilah would have been just as happy to never have had children. Not that she didn't love her kids, but Lilah's "maternal side" was narrow and not very deep. She'd always been more interested in her clubs and charities than she had in raising kids, leaving Megan, Paige and their brother Trace to be more or less raised by a succession of nannies. "I didn't see you come in."

"Not surprising," Lilah said, waving one elegant hand toward the open suitcase. "You have other things on your mind, don't you?"

Well-aimed thorns of guilt jabbed at her. "Yes, well, I would have told you about it, but you were at the fund-raiser this afternoon and—"

"Do you realize what sort of position this puts me in?"

Megan took a deep breath. "I know Father will be upset about my not marrying Willie, but—"

"Don't imagine for a moment that I'm concerned with your father's reaction to this," Lilah said, cutting her daughter off neatly.

People interrupted her all the time, Megan thought irritably. Why had she never noticed before? And of course her mother didn't care about Spencer's reaction. The two of them had been living separate lives under the same roof for years.

Taking a deep breath and blowing it out again slowly, Megan said again, "I am sorry, Mother."

Actually, she was sorry for a lot of things. Not least among them, the fact that she and her mother had never been close. But that ship had sailed years ago. No point in mourning it now.

"Please, Megan." Lilah's voice was cool. "If you had wanted me to know about your 'wedding,' you would have said something. What I want to know is, how long have you been planning it?"

"Uh…" Damn. She and Simon hadn't discussed this. Should she tell her family the truth? Admit that she was just his emergency wife? Sure, and then live with their knowing glances for the next year? No, she didn't think so. Besides, if she were to survive her father's fury over this, she'd have to convince *him* at least that this had been in the planning stages for at least a few weeks.

And to convince Spencer, she'd need Lilah to believe her, too. She wasn't an idiot. She knew her parents' marriage had stopped being about anything but convenience years ago. Growing up in a house, a child learned fast if his or her parents loved each other. And there'd never been that feeling in this house.

But if her mother believed her, then Lilah would stand up to Spencer, if only because she loved to see the man's plans thwarted.

"It was pretty sudden actually," Megan said and told herself that at least she wasn't lying. "He pretty much swept me off my feet."

One of Lilah's eyebrows lifted. "I find that hard to believe, Megan. You've never been one for spontaneity." She stood up, smoothed the front of her slacks, then stepped around the edge of the four-poster bed and stopped within a foot of her daughter. Staring at her, she said slowly, "But the damage is done, in any case. Have you given any thought at all to how this situation of yours will make me look to my friends?"

"What?" Megan watched her mother and noted the color suddenly rushing into her normally milk-pale cheeks.

"It will look as though you didn't want your own mother at your wedding, Megan," Lilah explained just in case her daughter had missed the point. "How am I to explain that to my friends?"

"I didn't mean to upset you, Mother." Megan curled her fingers into her palms and felt the impression of each of her nails digging into her skin.

The fact that she'd married a man her mother hadn't even met didn't seem to bother the woman. The real problem was how to stave off embarrassment in front of the ladies of the Napa League. For heaven's sake. Megan wasn't even sure why she was disappointed. Or angry.

She'd learned long ago that Lilah wasn't exactly the milk-and-cookies type of mother. She'd given birth to three kids and then calmly handed them off to be raised by people she *paid* to give them attention.

And yet, there was still a small corner of Megan's heart that ached to be loved. To be wanted. To have the sort of relationship with her parents that other people took for granted.

"You didn't think of me at all, you mean." Lilah spared her daughter a slight frown—and really, given her propensity for cosmetic injections, a slight frown was probably all she could manage. "I should think I deserved at least a little consideration."

"You're right." Megan heard herself saying the same words she always said when faced with a family confrontation. She always gave in. Always tried to smooth troubled waters. At least here at home.

Funny, but she never had any trouble taking on crabby caterers or furious florists. She could stand up for herself with her brother and sister. She'd had no trouble at all laying down the law to Simon Pearce.

But when it came to speaking her own mind to her

parents, she retreated into little-girl-Megan mode, trying and failing to please.

"Too little too late." Reaching up with one hand to unnecessarily smooth her still perfectly coiffed hair, Lilah stared at her for a long minute, then said, "I hope you know what you're doing, Megan."

"I do," she said, the repetition of her wedding vow echoing inside her head.

"Do you?" Lilah shook her head and, briefly, there was a glimmer of something in her eyes. Sympathy? Understanding? Whatever it was though, it was gone in a heartbeat. "I wonder. You do realize that you're leaving the home of one powerful man only to go to another man much like him."

Was Simon so much like her father? In the last few weeks, she'd worked closely with the man. Had come to know him—at least a bit. Yes, he was rich and powerful. But she hadn't noticed any of the coldness her father carried around inside him.

Megan had made her decision to marry Simon on instinct. And now she had to wonder if she'd jumped from the fire into the inferno.

"I wish you luck, Megan." With those few words, Lilah was finished. She turned and swept from the room, her head held regally high, her steps long and swift, showing her exasperation and displeasure all at once.

"That went well." Megan sighed, dropped onto the bed and let the silence seep into her bones. Her stomach churned and her head ached. Oh yes. This was just as she'd always imagined her wedding day. Fighting with her mother, avoiding her father and packing in solitude for a quick escape from the estate.

"Good God, Megan," she whispered. "What were you thinking?"

A short, sharp laugh shot from her throat and she pulled in a deep breath in a futile attempt to quiet the thousands of butterflies surging in her stomach. And, when that didn't work, she looked around her, trying to find comfort in familiar surroundings.

Her room hadn't changed much over the years. Well, except for getting rid of the shelves of dolls and replacing them with miles of books. Books she'd read and lived in. Books she'd pretended to be a part of when the reality of life as a poor little rich girl had become too much.

The walls were a pale green—a departure from the beige her mother insisted on throughout the house. The French doors opening onto her private balcony were open, and the soft March wind blew in, lifting the white sheers into a slow dance.

This one room in the Ashton estate was comfort. Home. Safety. She'd come here to hide as a girl when her parents' arguments became loud enough to travel up the wide staircase from the first floor. Years later, she'd come here to cry the night her father had told her that he'd bought off her last boyfriend.

And she'd dreamed here about having someone of her own. A husband. A family.

Now she had the husband, but it was nothing like she'd dreamed it would be. Was her mother right? Had she blindly walked into a marriage that was going to be the mirror image of her parents'?

And if so, how would she ever make it through the year they'd agreed on? Straightening her shoulders, Megan told herself that she didn't have to. She could back out now. What did it matter to her if the media clamored around Simon Pearce and hassled him about his 24-hour marriage?

Even as she considered it though, she remembered her father's threat to marry her off to Willie. Besides, she'd made a deal. Megan had never gone back on her word. Not to anyone. And she wasn't about to start now.

No matter how much she wanted to.

"Rough day?"

Her head snapped up and her gaze locked on Simon, standing in the open doorway of her bedroom. And suddenly, however her marriage had begun, now it looked like a lifeboat dropped into a stormy sea.

# Five

Simon's house wasn't as big as the estate.

But then, whose was?

From outside, the structure was a series of sharp angles made from weathered gray wood and glass. It looked forbidding and modern and completely out of touch with the gentle rolling green hillsides. But inside, Megan thought as her gaze slid across the foyer, was a whole different story.

Here, Simon's home looked warm, welcoming. Acres of gleaming wood floors led off in all directions and she peeked in at the rooms she passed on her way to the stairs. Overstuffed sofas and chairs, muted throw rugs, well-polished wood furniture, Tiffany lamps, their stained-glass shades shining jewel-colored splashes of light on their surroundings. Everything about the place whispered comfort. A far cry from the estate—where the first rule she and her siblings had learned was *don't touch*.

She shifted her gaze to Simon, carrying her suit-case, as he led the way upstairs. The stair balustrade was deeply carved, with pine boughs and flowers twining the railing as if they were springing to life right out of the wood. Framed paintings lined the pale yellow walls and the stair runner picked up the yellow in narrow stripes of faded cream.

The ticking of a grandfather clock at the foot of the stairs followed after them, like a heartbeat sounding out each step.

"It's pretty," she said lamely, more to combat the silence of the big house than for any other reason.

"Thanks." He turned right at the head of the stairs and stalked along a wide, well-lit hallway, with Megan hot on his heels.

When he stepped into the master suite, Megan stopped in the doorway to simply stare. Very male, the room was dominated by a four-poster bed big enough to play softball on. Megan swallowed hard and told herself she should be glad of the bed's size. She could hug one edge and hope Simon stayed on the other. At least for the week she had coming to her.

And when that week was up? A tingle of anticipation zapped her and Megan tried not to shiver.

Good heavens, what had she gotten herself into? *Stop thinking about the bed.*

The rest of the room was furnished simply, but tastefully. A wide bank of windows made up one wall and the view was amazing—she could see practically the whole valley stretched out below her. Cushioned window seats with plump pillows beckoned daydreamers, and a cozy love seat rested in front of a brick fireplace, its hearth cold at the moment.

She moved into the room as Simon tossed her suitcase onto the bed and she caught a glimpse of the master bath—miles of sky-blue tiles and a tub big enough to host the softball team when they finished their game on the giant bed. Oh boy.

"Feeling better?"

She shook herself out of her thoughts and slanted a look at the man watching her. "As opposed to what?"

One corner of his mouth lifted then flattened out again. "You weren't looking so hot when we left your house."

"Gee, thanks. What every bride longs to hear."

"Look," he said, stuffing his hands into his pockets as he walked toward her. "I know this hasn't been an easy day—"

"It's been an *interesting* day."

He kept walking, one long stride at a time until he was standing just inches from her. His cologne reached her, some musky scent that seemed to dive right for the pit of her stomach and beyond. Whoa. Okay, she needed to get a grip.

His eyes, the color of coastal fog, stared at her and she felt herself nearly being hypnotized by them. She couldn't look away. Didn't want to. And what did that mean for heaven's sake?

Several long moments ticked past and she was struck again by the silence in the big house. At home, there was always something going on. People talking, shouting, music drifting from either her room or Paige's. Trace had his television on, with those annoying sports-announcer voices dribbling into the hallways.

But here, she was pretty sure if she opened the window, she'd be able to hear grass growing.

It gave her the heebie-jeebies.

"Is it always this quiet?" she asked suddenly.

He paused, cocked his head as if listening, then shrugged. "Yeah, I guess so. Why?"

"Don't you think it's a little...eerie?"

He laughed. Shortly, harshly, as if he wasn't used to laughing and Megan wouldn't have been surprised if that were true. A shame, she thought, because laughter did great things for his eyes. And his mouth. And—never mind.

"Worried about ghosts?" he asked.

"No," she snapped back, just a little irritated. "I'm just not used to all this quiet."

"You'll get used to it," he assured her.

"Or I'll find a way to fix it," she told him.

One eyebrow lifted as he studied her. "This is going to be a long year, isn't it?"

Now Megan smiled for the first time since that morning. "You betcha."

Simon watched his new wife move around the kitchen and was amazed at how much at home she seemed. She'd changed into a pale green T-shirt and white shorts that displayed her long, tanned legs to an incredible advantage. Not that he was noticing or anything. "I would have thought an Ashton wouldn't know one end of a toaster from the other."

She shot him a quick look over her shoulder as she rummaged in the stainless steel refrigerator. "My brother and sister and I all learned our way around the kitchen early." She straightened up again, her arms full of bacon, eggs and bags of vegetables. Slamming the fridge door shut with her hip, she carried her booty to the granite island in the middle of the room.

Standing on the opposite side of the counter from him, she unloaded her things and grinned. Simon's breath caught in his chest and he had to remind himself to breathe. Why hadn't he noticed her smile before? During the last few weeks they'd worked together more than a dozen times and yet, that smile had never hit him quite so hard before.

Then it dawned on him.

Working with him rarely induced people to smile.

"I'm not saying we're great chefs or anything," Megan was saying as she broke several eggs into a cobalt-blue mixing bowl. "But if left to our own devices in a kitchen, we wouldn't starve."

"Your mother taught you then?" he asked, remembering his own mother insisting that he learn to cook—saying she wouldn't have his future wife blaming her for raising a helpless man.

Megan laughed again. "Oops. Sorry." She shrugged as she grated cheese and then added it to the mixture of eggs she'd already whipped into a froth. "But the thought of my mother willingly walking into a kitchen just struck me as funny." She shrugged. "Our cook taught the three of us. We used to spend a lot of time in the kitchen. You know, after school or in the summer…"

"You enjoyed it." It wasn't a question. He could see it in her eyes.

"Sure. What kid wouldn't? Being able to make a mess and play with fire?" She grinned again and Simon felt the same punch of awareness slam into him. And even as he savored the sensation, he reminded himself that this was not a *real* marriage. That they'd both come into this unusual arrangement knowing that it would end in a year.

Still, he reasoned, that didn't mean he couldn't enjoy the year while it was here, did it?

Rummaging around in the drawers of the island,

she found the knife she was looking for, then went to work on the vegetables. Broccoli, bell peppers and mushrooms fell beneath the quickly moving blade until she was satisfied. Then she reached up to the wrought-iron cage above the island and pulled at a copper-bottomed pot.

As she did, the hem of her tight T-shirt lifted, baring her belly button and enough smooth, tanned skin to make Simon curl his hands into fists to keep from reaching for her. Instead, he got up abruptly, went to the fridge and opened it. "Want a beer?"

Megan finally freed the skillet she'd been working on and dropped back down. Slanting him a look, she said, "You're asking an Ashton…of Ashton Estates and Winery if she wants a *beer?*"

"Yeah."

She nodded. "Just checking. And yes, I would."

He smiled to himself as she walked to the eight-burner stove built into a wall of honey oak cabinets. Slapping the skillet onto a burner, she dropped a slice of butter into the pan and melted it before adding the eggs, cheese and vegetables.

"Now," she said, pausing for a sip of the beer, "I don't want you getting used to this kind of treatment." Glancing at him, she continued. "I make a great omelet, but that's not to say I'm going to cook one every night."

He cradled his beer between his palms and looked at her. Her wide green eyes sparkled in the overhead light and her hair fell in a long, thick ponytail to just below her shoulders. She smelled like summer and smiled like a devil. She was going to torture him, he could feel it coming. He told himself he never should have agreed to that whole one-week getting-to-know-each-other-thing. Who said you had to know a person before having great sex?

And just looking at her told him the sex would be incredible.

His body went hard and tight and he had to fight for control. Something that hadn't happened to him since he was a kid. Simon Pearce wasn't a man to be led around by his hormones for God's sake.

When he finally spoke, his voice was harder than he'd planned—but hell, it was her own fault. Why'd she have to look so damn good?

"I've got a cook, Megan. I didn't marry you for your culinary talents."

The smile faded from her face and she took another drink of beer before setting the bottle down on the blue-tile counter. Picking up a wooden spoon, she stirred the egg mixture until the vegetables were evenly distributed, then turned the fire down and faced him.

"If you've got a cook, why am I doing this?"

He scowled and took another drink of beer, hoping the cold, frothy liquid would wash away the knot in his throat. "Because I gave her and the housekeeper two weeks off. I was supposed to be in Fiji, remember?"

"Oh. Right." She glanced at the pan on the stove and, apparently satisfied, left it and walked toward him. "So for the next two weeks, it's just you and I in this house?"

"Yep."

"Alone."

"Yep."

She sighed. "Well, I hope you know how to call out for pizza."

Simon smiled. "I think I can handle that."

Megan nodded. "Then we should survive."


Megan lay in the dark and watched moonlight play on the ceiling.

Weird.

She tugged the hem of her short silk nightgown down over her thighs, turned her head on the pillow and stared into the shadows, trying to make out Simon's profile in the gloom. But since he was clear on the other side of a bed the size of the European continent, it wasn't easy.

She wondered if he was still awake.

Wondered if he was wearing pajamas or—gulp—sleeping nude?

She wondered why she was wondering.

She wondered if you could go crazy just from thinking too much.

"You're awake, aren't you?"

His deep voice shattered the quiet and startled

Megan enough that she gasped in a breath. "Sorry. You scared me."

"How?" he asked, and she heard the amusement in his voice. "You knew I was here."

"Yeah, but the bed's so big, it sounded like your voice was coming from the next county."

"I like plenty of room," he said.

She kept her gaze fixed on the moonlit ceiling and told herself she really shouldn't think about why he liked all that room. Had he had teams of cheerleaders in here? All at once?

As if he could hear her thoughts, he said wryly, "I move around a lot in my sleep."

"Uh-huh." She wasn't convinced.

The silk sheets rustled and she felt a tug, so she clamped her arms at her sides to hold the slippery sheets in place.

"Worried?" he asked.

There was that amusement again, Megan thought and scowled to herself.

"Should I be?" she countered, shifting her gaze from the ceiling to the bank of windows and the star-filled sky beyond. "I mean, you did promise to give me a week."

"I did."

"Is your word any good?"

"It is," he insisted, despite the fact that the silk sheets moved and pulled again.

He was coming closer.

She knew it.

Even though, with a bed this size, it might take him all night to edge his way over to her side, Megan sucked in a deep gulp of air and held it.

"So you're not sneaking over here in the dark, then?"

"Sneaking?" he repeated, and didn't his voice sound a lot closer now? "No. Moving, yes."

"Well, cut it out." She inched a little bit more toward the edge of the bed. Much farther though and her whole right side would be hanging off the mattress, and wouldn't that make a pretty picture?

"Nervous?"

Oh yeah. He was definitely closer.

She could smell his cologne again.

And his musky scent that was somehow comforting and mysterious all at once was doing something very strange to her insides. Because it's dark, she told herself. Everything is different at night. Sights. Smells. Instincts.

She knew this because her instincts were, at the moment, screaming at her to turn *toward* him, not away. She'd been getting those little spirally feelings about him ever since dinner. Sitting across from each other at a granite counter and sharing beer and omelet had somehow been...cozy. And every time he smiled, she felt the same punch of something dizzying sweep through her.

And now that they were alone. In a bed the size of an ocean. Well, instincts were hard to fight.

Still, she tried.

"Why would I be nervous?" she countered and hoped that her voice really hadn't creaked on that last word.

"We *are* married, you know," he said, and this time, his voice was just an arm's reach away.

She did *not* reach.

"Yes," she agreed, trying to hold on to the slippery silk sheets despite his attempts to pull at them. "But we agreed to no sex for a week."

"Who said anything about sex?" he asked.

Megan closed her eyes and gulped. His voice was a whisper of temptation in the shadows. The night closed in tight around them and she swore she could hear her own heartbeat crashing like a bass drum.

"Then what are you talking about?"

"Just," he said as he slid up next to her, stopping just short of touching her, "being close."

Megan laughed and her nervousness disappeared in a flash. "Oh, boy, I haven't heard that one since junior high."

He stopped moving closer and she could almost hear the insult in his voice. "Excuse me?"

Ridiculous, but the affront in his tone had her relaxing. Loosening her grip on the silky sheets, she turned onto her side and finally looked at him. She was only mildly surprised that they were nearly nose to nose.

"Close?" she repeated, smiling. "You just want to

be close? Is that along the lines of 'we don't have to do anything, I just want to hold you'? Or is it more like 'I won't do anything you don't *want* me to do'?"

He frowned at her. "I only meant that we don't have to sleep on the edges of a very big bed to avoid having sex."

"True," Megan said, studying his face as well as she could in the moonlight. But his gray eyes were more shadowed now, almost unreadable and his expression was closed. "I think I can restrain myself—and *you.*"

His jaw worked as he studied her and she wondered what it was he was trying so hard not to say. But she'd probably never know, since he took a deep breath, blew it out in a rush and said, "You don't have to worry. I don't force myself on women."

Okay, she'd insulted him and she really hadn't meant to. But jeez, he was really encroaching on her personal space and the fact that she didn't really mind was especially irritating.

"I didn't mean that."

"What did you mean?"

"Just—oh for heaven's sake, I didn't mean anything, okay?"

"Good." He jammed his pillow up beneath his neck, sighed and then closed his eyes.

Megan watched him for several seconds before whispering, "What are you doing?"

He opened one eye. "Going to sleep."

"Um...don't you think you should move back to your own side of the continent?"

His mouth curved. "No. I'm comfortable."

She just stared at him for a long minute, but he didn't open his eyes again and in seconds, his breathing was deep, even, telling her he was sleeping.

"Well," she murmured, "at least *one* of us is comfy."

# Six

The next couple of days slipped past in a rush.

Megan managed to avoid any confrontations with her father simply because he was nowhere to be seen. He left the estate before Megan arrived for work and returned long after she left.

Which should have calmed her down a little.

Instead, it had the opposite effect.

She felt like a turkey the day before Thanksgiving—on edge and waiting for the ax to fall.

And Simon was being no help at all.

She couldn't relax at work because she was just too busy—not to mention keeping a wary eye out for her father. And she couldn't relax at "home," because Simon was *everywhere.*

At least that's how it felt.

If she took a swim in the pool, she climbed out to find him standing there holding a towel for her. If she took a walk in the garden, he was right behind her. If she tried to sleep in that gigantic bed, he slipped across the mattress to lie right beside her, *guaranteeing* she wouldn't be nodding off.

But tonight, for the first time since her all-too-hasty marriage, Megan had the big wood-and-glass house to herself. Simon was working late—he'd left a message for her on the answering machine saying he didn't know when he'd be home. And if she felt a small stir of disappointment, she told herself it was only because she was now used to having him dog her every footstep.

So to prove to herself that she was indeed enjoying the solitude, Megan cranked up the CD player and let a little classic rock and roll vibrate through the empty house. Then she went into the master bath, dumped a gallon of bubble bath into the massive tub and turned on the faucets. While jasmine-scented bubbles stirred the surface and steam lifted to fog the mirrors, Megan stripped out of her work clothes and dropped everything onto the cool sky-blue tiles. Then she picked up the bottle of brute cuvée sparkling wine, which she'd liberated from the tasting room on the estate, and poured herself a glass. With the first sip, she smiled and breathed a relaxed sigh.

Setting the glass down on the countertop, she looked into the mirror and watched herself scoop her hair onto the top of her head and pin it into place. Then, grinning, she picked up her glass of wine and stepped into a tub made for a queen.

Hot water still rushed into the tub, and as she settled herself, Megan felt the strain of the last couple of days drain away. Cool wine, hot water and the soothing scent of jasmine. Everything a girl could need.

"Okay," she murmured, having another sip, "not *everything*." And just like that, her thoughts returned to the man who was her husband. Her brain had been doing that a lot lately, she realized. While talking on the phone to suppliers or caterers, she caught herself doodling Simon's name on a pad of paper. While talking a nervous bride through her first visit to the reception hall, she remembered her own walk down that aisle and the look on Simon's face just before he'd kissed her.

Her body stirred uncomfortably and she shifted, sliding down deeper into the frothy water. Scowling now, she said, "It doesn't mean anything. Of course you're a little itchy. You're sleeping beside a naked man every night."

She groaned tightly and remembered the morning after their wedding when Simon had tossed back the covers and walked across the room stark naked. It had taken every ounce of her willpower not to call him back and demand he do incredible things to her body.

"Oh man." Megan gulped at the wine to ease her suddenly dry throat. It didn't help.

As the water sluiced over her skin, she sat up, leaned forward and shut off the taps. Now there was just the slosh of the water around her and the music surging from the other room. She tipped her head back and stared out the bay window beside her at the night. The first time she'd showered in here, she'd worried about giving a peep show to whoever might have a handy telescope.

But Simon had reassured her, saying that they were on top of a hill in the middle of thirty acres— so her privacy was ensured in the second-story bathroom. And now that she could relax about it, Megan had to admit that it felt a little decadent to be naked in front of an uncurtained window.

"Okay, either too much wine or not enough," she muttered and looked over at the bottle sitting where she'd left it on the counter. "Damn it."

"Thirsty?"

"Whoops!" Megan shouted and slid beneath the veil of bubbles, all the while glaring at the doorway. Simon grinned and leaned one shoulder against the doorjamb. "You scared me to death."

He straightened and shrugged off his suit jacket, tossing it behind him into the bedroom. "You would have heard me if you didn't have the music on so loud."

She stretched out one hand and gathered in a few more bubbles, arranging them strategically over her still-submerged body. "You could have said something."

"I did."

"Oh. Right."

He smiled and held up the bottle. "More wine?"

"Yeah, please." Carefully, she held up her glass, keeping a wary eye on the bubble front.

"I'll join you if you don't mind."

"Sure," she said, thinking there was plenty of wine to go around.

He refilled her glass, then left the room and came back with another for himself. After filling it to the rim, he took a sip, smiled his approval. "Not bad."

"We, of Ashton Estates and Winery, thank you," she said, lifting her glass in salute. "This is our most popular wine, you know," she continued, hoping to fill the silence even if she was only talking about wine. "People buy it by the vat load and—what're you doing?"

Setting his glass down on the counter, Simon unbuttoned his shirt and yanked the hem of it out of his trousers.

"Simon?" Megan kept one eye on him and the other on her quickly dissipating blanket of bubbles.

"Joining you," he said and undid his belt, then the button and zipper of his slacks. "You said you didn't mind."

"Joining me in the wine," she said quickly, holding up her glass and pointing at it for emphasis. "The *wine*."

He picked up his glass, took a sip, then studied it, frowning. "Not enough room for both of us in there."

"Very funny."

"But there's plenty of room in there," he said, nodding at the tub.

Her body sizzled.

Whoa.

Megan gulped in air and when that didn't help, gulped down more wine. Good heavens. She hadn't meant—didn't think he'd—but now he—*help me*.

He undressed quickly, dropping his clothes onto the floor to join her own discarded heap of clothing. Megan closed her eyes, telling herself it was way safer that way.

But she peeked anyway.

Couldn't help herself.

And she was willing to challenge *any* woman to be able to look away from a body like Simon's.

He was tall and lean, yet well muscled. His abdomen was a sharply defined six-pack and his chest was broad, tanned and only lightly dusted with black hair. His hips were narrow, his legs long and his—she swallowed another mouthful of wine. *Oh, boy.*

Simon picked up his wineglass and stepped over the edge of the tub. He winced and hissed in a breath. "I didn't know you were trying to boil yourself alive."

She shrugged, then scooped more bubbles up to

her neck in a futile attempt to hide the body he'd already gotten plenty glimpses of. "I like hot water."

"There's hot, and then there's simmering," he muttered, sliding carefully into the water on the opposite side of the tub from her. As he quickly became accustomed to the heat though, he had to admit it felt great. Ordinarily, he wasn't the kind of guy to go for jasmine-scented bubbles—or baths, for that matter—but he was up for something new. Something…*interesting.*

"I thought you were going to work late," she said, gulping at her wine.

"I was," he admitted, then frowned to himself. He'd had every intention of staying at the office most of the night. But thoughts of Megan had haunted him, making concentration impossible. How was a man supposed to think about bottom lines when he couldn't get a certain woman's *bottom* out of his mind?

This had never happened to him before.

He thrived on control.

Simon Pearce ruled his universe.

He took another slug of the cold wine and let it slide down his throat. Then his gaze shifted to his wife. The woman who had moved into his house and upset his routine. The woman he wanted under him, over him, around him. The woman he fantasized about making love to.

The woman who was making him nuts.

"So how's work?" she asked.

"Great." One word, ground out of a suddenly tight throat.

"Yeah, me, too."

He frowned thoughtfully. "Have you heard from your father yet?"

"No," she said and tried to shrug the thought aside, but he saw the glitter in her eyes that told him she was worried. "I don't know what he's waiting for either."

"Maybe he's not as upset as you thought he'd be."

She laughed shortly, but there was no humor in it. Only more worry. "Trust me, that's not it."

"So why would he wait?"

"To up the tension," she muttered reluctantly. "That's how Spencer Ashton maneuvers." She frowned and sipped at her wine again. "'Keep your opponent off guard,' that's his number one rule. And he uses it even with his family. Heck," she corrected herself, "*especially* with his family. He's always been like this and I fall for it every time." She slapped the bathwater and sloshed a mini wave over the edge of the dark blue tub. "Instead of putting it out of my mind, I fret about it and think about it and in general drive myself nuts long before Father can lower his boom."

Simon's brain whipped through memories of his own childhood and mentally compared his parents to hers. Or at least, their fathers. Simon's father had been a great guy. Good father, honest businessman and devoted husband. All in all, a hard act to follow—which was probably why he'd taken so long to decide to get married. And why, when he did make the decision, he'd chosen a woman who didn't have high expectations of love. Because damn it, he didn't like the idea of divorce. Even though he'd walked right into marriage with Megan with a divorce all neatly laid out for them at the end of a year.

But, he thought now, that year-end was a long way away and for the moment, he was in a bathtub, with his wife. Maybe he couldn't help her with the worries clogging her mind, but with very little effort, he should be able to take her mind off of it for a while. He stretched out his legs and his foot brushed her hip.

She jerked upright, giving him a brief but tantalizing glimpse of her peaked pink nipples. Then she was underwater again, glaring at him. "Hey! Personal space!"

"It's a tub, Megan," he drawled slowly. "There's not enough room for personal space."

"It's a big tub," she countered, narrowing her eyes at him.

"Big enough," he allowed.

Her eyes went to slits. "Big enough for what?"

"All kinds of things."

"Okay, bath time over," she announced, then added, "close your eyes."

He grinned, laid one arm on the rim of the tub and lifted his glass for another sip. "I don't think so."

"What?"

"I said, if you want to get out of the tub right now, you'll have to do it with an audience."

She inhaled sharply, deeply, and Simon thought, if looks could kill, he'd be dead, buried and his grave danced over.

"Not much of a gentleman, are you?"

"Nope." But damn, he was enjoying himself.

She grumbled something he was probably better off not hearing, then glanced to where her robe hung on the back of the door, more than six feet away. Apparently, she was trying to figure out just how good a look he'd get at her if she made a run for it.

"Why don't we just sit here and relax together?" he suggested, shifting his legs and moving along the circumference of the tub, inching closer to her.

"You're inching," she accused.

"Who, me?" Yep. Really enjoying himself. And he couldn't remember the last time he'd smiled this much.

Megan blew out a breath and drained the last of her wine. Holding her glass out, she said simply, "More."

Simon nodded, reached over the edge of the tub for the bottle and topped both glasses off. Then he set the bottle back down and moved in closer—as he'd been planning to do all along.

The woman tormented him without even trying.

She was acting like a reluctant virgin and had him behaving like a cartoon villain.

He really liked it.

She watched him. "You're inching again."

"No, now I'm actually sliding."

"Why?" she asked.

"Are you serious?"

She blew out a breath. "Okay, fine. I *know* why. But we agreed to a week to get to know each other."

He smiled slowly and watched her teeth tug at her bottom lip. Amazingly enough, he felt that tug all the way to the tips of his toes. "What better way to get to know each other than by sharing a bath?"

"Oh I don't know...*bowling?*"

He chuckled and slid up beside her, pulling her close. The hot water rushed around them, slapping at them, caressing them. "We're not dressed for bowling."

"Seriously Simon..."

"Why be serious now?" he asked, dipping his head closer, closer. He tasted her. One quick nip of her mouth that left his senses reeling and sent his heartbeat into overdrive. His body went rock hard and needy, and the pulse point at the base of her throat jittered as if she knew exactly what she was doing to him.

"Because," she said, leaning her head back against his arm and staring up into his eyes. "We made a deal and—"

"The deal was, no *sex.*"

"You've really got to stop interrupting me."

He grinned. "Sorry. What were you going to say?"

"Uh..." She stared up into his eyes. "About what?"

He set his wineglass on the wide edge of the tub

and dropped his free hand into the water. He just wanted to touch her. *Had* to feel the soft silk of her skin. He needed it more than his next breath. Wanted it more than anything he'd ever wanted in his life.

And couldn't have stopped if there'd been a gun to his head.

He cupped her breast, thumbing her nipple and Megan sighed, arching into him and tipping the rest of her wine into the water.

"Simon…"

"This isn't sex," he reminded her, his voice a soft hush, barely heard over the slosh of the water as she moved. "This is just touching."

"Yeah," she said on a sigh, "but…"

"Let me touch you," he whispered, dipping his head to where her nipple just crested the surface of the water. He took the small pink bud into his mouth, tasting her, teasing her. But it backfired on him.

Not only was he tormenting her.

He was driving himself over the edge.

One taste would never be enough.

"Simon, oh, don't stop…."

Her voice, in breathy little gasps, fired his body and punched his emotions. As he suckled her, he trailed his free hand through the water, down the length of her body, skimming across her skin with the lightest of touches, while she moved and groaned beneath him. Every instinct clamored at him to grab her, hold her tight, bury himself inside her and push them both toward an explosion of pleasure.

Instead though, he corralled his own needs and focused on the soft slide of her skin against his. On the delicious curves and valleys of her body. On the hush of her sighs in the jasmine-scented air.

He drew on her nipple and felt her hand sweep up to cup the back of his head, holding him to her as if she were afraid he'd stop. But he wouldn't. Couldn't. He wanted more. He wanted *all*.

Her hips lifted in the water as his hand found her center. He covered her with his palm and felt her heat rise up to meet him. He groaned and ran the edges of his teeth across her nipple. She moved again, twisting slightly, the cooling water sloshing high and over the edge of the tub.

Then he slipped one finger into her warmth and she moaned softly, gently. So he pushed another finger inside her and as he plunged her depths, his thumb caressed the small, sensitive core of her until she trembled in his grasp.

Her hands tightened on him. Short, neat nails scraped his back even while she held his head to her breast. She groaned, arching high into his touch, rocking her hips, climbing a peak he'd taken her to.

He felt the wracking shudders that rippled through her and held her close as she soared over the edge of want and shouted his name as she fell.

* * *

Megan's skin was all pruny, she had a bruise on her knee from slamming it into the side of the tub and she'd pulled a muscle in her neck.

And she'd never felt better.

She practically skipped down the staircase, wrapped up in her plush forest-green robe. She felt warm and loose and should have been completely ashamed of herself for how she'd spent the last hour.

But she wasn't.

She hit the bottom of the stairs and did a quick little two-step toward the hall that would take her to the kitchen. After all, she was *married,* right? If she wanted to let her husband take her to the stars and back again, while sitting in a bathtub the size of an Olympic pool—God, she wanted to go back upstairs and do it all again.

"Megan," she muttered, "you're shameless. Aren't you lucky?"

While Simon was upstairs, showering off the jasmine bubbles, she was headed for the kitchen to take out plates and more wine. Her thoughtful, very talented husband had already called for pizza, and right now, Megan thought she could probably eat the delivery guy's car.

She was halfway down the hall, still enjoying the shivery leftovers still humming through her body, when the doorbell sounded out and she slid to a stop. "Wow," she said, turning for the door and doubling back. "When they say under thirty minutes, those pizza guys aren't kidding."

She ran down the hall and would have tried sliding, but her bare feet wouldn't have slid on the wood floor anyway. The doorbell pealed again, so she hurried, wondering why the pizza man was in a bigger rush than his customers.

Making a mental note to try sliding down that long hall with socks on one day soon, Megan yelled up the stairs to Simon, "Pizza guy's here, bring your wallet, my prince!"

Then she threw open the door and came face-to-face with her father.

# Seven

Simon headed downstairs, wearing only the slacks he'd hurriedly dragged on when he heard Megan shout. Already pulling a twenty from his wallet to pay for the pizza, he stopped halfway down the staircase and watched Spencer Ashton step into the house.

Soft light from the overhead chandelier danced over the man and his daughter, and the breeze slipping through the still-open door lifted Megan's hair from the collar of her robe. She looked pale and uneasy, her fingers nervously smoothing the edges of her robe, fiddling with the cloth belt around her narrow waist.

"What do you think you're doing?" Spencer demanded and Simon moved one step farther down the staircase. The older man either didn't notice him or didn't care. He didn't even give Megan a chance to speak before he answered his own question. "Do you really think I'll allow you to defy me this way?"

"I wasn't trying to defy you." Megan took one long step back from her father and Simon went on red alert. Every protective instinct he had clicked in and only revved up as Spencer stared his daughter down and continued talking.

"I waited for you to come to your senses," the man growled and his deep voice reverberated through the house like a dank, thick fog. "Two days. Two days, Megan, and you didn't come to apologize."

"Apologize?" she echoed.

"Finally, it became apparent that that wasn't going to happen."

"I'm glad you understand, Father—" Megan stiffened her shoulders and lifted her chin. She swung her hair back from her face and Simon felt a stab of pride. She looked like a damn queen, even in a dark green bathrobe.

"On the contrary. There is nothing about this I *understand.*" Spencer's eyes narrowed and his features went grim. "Your sudden marriage is nothing more than the act of a rebellious child."

*"Child?"*

Simon heard the outrage in Megan's voice and wondered why in the hell her father couldn't.

"You listen to me, Megan." The older man shook one finger at her as if it were a pointer in the hands of a surly teacher. "I want you to pack your things. I'll take you home, start the annulment procedures tomorrow and by the end of the week, this marriage will be forgotten. Senator Jackson owes me a favor or two. He can expedite things."

"So I can marry his son?" Megan's hands clenched and dropped to her sides.

"Of course. As we'd planned." Spencer checked his watch as if he'd already wasted enough of his time on this.

Simon gritted his teeth. Neither of the Ashtons had noticed he was there, listening. And though he wanted to rush downstairs and ride to the rescue, he also wanted to hear what Megan had to say. Would she cave in to her father's demands, or would she honor the agreement they'd made?

"I can't do that," she said and her voice got firmer with every word. "No, I *won't* do that."

The man looked as surprised as he would have been if a dog had suddenly told him to go fetch his own stick. "I beg your pardon?"

"I said I won't leave my husband."

"Your *husband*." Spencer snorted. "You don't even know the man."

"I've known him for six weeks, Father," Megan retorted and instead of backing up again, she actually moved in a little closer to her father. "I met him at the estate while I was planning…" Her voice trailed off.

Simon smiled to himself. She wasn't about to admit that they'd *met* while she was planning his wedding to someone else. And it was only then he realized that she was right. They *had* known each other for six weeks. He'd watched her do her job, balancing her skills with organization and her ability to soothe people in already tense situations.

Hell. She'd stood up to *him*. And not many people were able to say that. He liked her. More than that, he respected her. Still, he wanted to shout encouragement, but he also didn't want to distract her.

"I'm married, Father," she said. "You're just going to have to deal with it. Simon's my husband and he's going to stay that way."

That was all he needed to hear. Simon cleared his throat and when the two people in the foyer turned to look at him, he started down the stairs again and gave Spencer a stiff smile. "Good of you to drop by," he said, as he moved to stand beside Megan.

Spencer breathed deeply, quickly and the color in his face darkened furiously. "This is no social call."

"Then why don't you explain to me exactly why you're here, in *our* house, shouting at *my* wife?" Simon dropped one arm around Megan's shoulders and pulled her close. She leaned into him as if grateful for the support.

"Your wife." Spencer nearly snorted the words.

"I'm here," he said, dismissing his daughter and focusing his fury on Simon, "to end this charade. Megan is engaged to the son of an old friend of mine and I intend to see to it that that marriage takes place."

Simon laughed. He knew it was the one thing that could either deflate or enrage an opponent and at the moment, he didn't care which effect it had on the man. He didn't like Spencer Ashton. He'd heard enough rumors and innuendos over the years to make it a point to steer clear of him. And the last few minutes had convinced him that had been a good decision. "Since Megan's already married, I don't see the point of this visit. You're wasting your time and ours."

"You forget who the hell you're dealing with, Pearce," Spencer said, his already florid face ruddy with temper. A vein throbbed in his temple as he shot a glance at his daughter. "Megan is my daughter. She'll do as she's told. This situation will be taken care of."

"Just a darn minute, Father." Megan wrapped one arm around Simon's waist as if holding onto a talisman. "I'll do what I please. I'm not a child anymore and you don't run my life."

"I beg your pardon?"

If Ashton's voice had been any colder, Simon thought, he would have been spitting ice cubes.

Megan sailed right on—only the tight grip of her fingers against his bare skin letting him know how much she hated doing this in front of him. "I told you I wouldn't marry Willie. Now, I'm married to Simon. And there's nothing you can do about it."

Simon squeezed her shoulders in solidarity, then shifted his gaze from his wife's stony profile to the man still glaring at him. "You have your answer. And that should take care of any business you had here," he said. "So I think you should be leaving."

Spencer's eyebrows shot up and his eyes widened in shock. "You're asking me to leave?"

"No," Simon corrected and silently congratulated himself on keeping a rein on his temper. "I'm *telling* you to leave."

"You son of a bitch, if you think you can—"

Exasperated, Megan blew out a breath. "Father—"

Simon pushed her behind him and hoped she'd stay there. He wasn't looking forward to planting his fist in his wife's father's face, but if he had to, he wanted her out of the line of fire.

Just then, another car pulled up in the long circular driveway and parked, motor running. An electric pizza sign on its roof blinked red and white and its horn tooted a greeting.

"Our dinner's arrived," Simon said, and taking advantage of Spencer's surprise, stepped forward and took the man by the elbow to steer him toward the doorway. The older man didn't let him get away with that for long, though.

He yanked his arm free, sent his daughter a look

of frustrated fury, then glared at Simon again. "This isn't over."

"It's long past over." Simon had had enough.

He dealt with powerful men every day. He was used to the egos, the confidence and the arrogance. Had even been accused of being fairly arrogant himself. He'd built Pearce Industries into a conglomerate worth millions by knowing how to defuse a situation and how to bend when necessary. But never once in all of his negotiations had he ever entertained the notion of plowing his fist into another man's face.

Until today.

Watching emotions churn in his wife's eyes, hearing her father talk to her as though she were a low-level employee made Simon want to throw the man out on his ear. And even while he was forced to choke down the urges, a part of him was stunned with the force of the need to protect that was choking him.

"I suggest you go home, Mr. Ashton," Simon murmured through gritted teeth. He kept his voice low, so that only Spencer heard him. "And don't you *ever* come into *our* home and bully my wife again."

The older man met his gaze for a long moment and Simon found himself hoping the bastard would try to throw a punch. But that wasn't Spencer Ashton's way. Even furious, the man retained complete control of whatever emotions he allowed himself.

"Yo!" Behind Spencer, the pizza delivery kid

bounded up the narrow brick walkway and rocked on his heels. "Somebody in this place call for pizza?"

"We did," Simon said, sparing the kid a look before turning his stare back on Spencer. "Are we clear?"

The older man's jaw worked as if he were grinding to bits the angry words he wanted to spit out. "We're clear, Pearce."

Simon smiled tightly. "Thanks for stopping by."

"Cool car, dude." The kid was eyeing Spencer's low-slung European sports car with envy etched into his face.

"Get out of my way." Spencer nearly bowled the boy over in his fury.

"Jeez, chill why don'cha?" The boy with long blond hair and dimples shrugged off Spencer, handed the pizza to Simon and said, "Eighteen ninety-five—not including tip."

"Right." Simon gave him twenty-five dollars and closed the door on the kid's burbled thanks. Turning to face Megan, he looked into her eyes, and not knowing exactly what else to say after the set-to with her father, said only, "Pizza smells good."

She inhaled sharply, blew the air out again in a rush, and stared at him for a long moment before grinning. "My hero."

His heart swelled. He should have laughed it off. She probably hadn't meant it as any more than a joke. But instead, those two simple words ricocheted around inside Simon's chest until they pinged into his heart and heated him clear through. He'd never been anyone's hero before and damned if he didn't like it. "Your father'll get over it, Megan."

She shook her head, but she was still smiling. "No he won't. But it doesn't matter. Not anymore. I'm just glad the confrontation's done. I do want you to know though, that I could have handled him. I've been doing it on my own for years."

"I know," he said and shifted his grip on the pizza box. He'd seen her gearing up for the argument. Had witnessed her putting up defenses she'd no doubt spent a lifetime designing. And he couldn't really explain what had driven him to step in. Couldn't even explain it to himself. All he knew for sure was that the driving urge inside him that had demanded he defend his wife had been the most overpowering sensation he'd ever known. "I just couldn't stand there and let you take the hit for a marriage that was all my idea in the first place."

She laughed shortly. "You didn't exactly drag me to the altar by the hair, you know. Like I just told my father. I make my own choices, Simon. If I hadn't wanted to marry you, I wouldn't have."

He inhaled sharply as she moved in closer. The scent of Italian spices and tomato sauce was thick, yet he managed to catch a whiff of the jasmine-scented bubble bath still clinging to her skin. Instantly, his body hardened at the reminders of what they'd been doing upstairs just a few short minutes ago. And the images of what he'd like to be doing right now.

"I just wanted to help," he said, forcing the words past a knot the size of a football lodged in his throat.

"I know," Megan said and moved even closer to him, looking up at him through wide green eyes that looked as clear and sharp as the first grasses of summer. "That's why I'm saying thank you. I've never had anyone stand beside me like that before. I liked it."

She smiled again and his heart turned over. He wondered how in the hell a simple smile could pack such a punch.

Simon's throat was tight. "I won't let him—or anyone else—talk to you like that."

"I know that, too," she said and reached up to cup his cheek in her palm. "And it feels really…*good*, to have someone with me. To not be on my own. I mean, I didn't actually *need* the cavalry, but I was really glad when it—you—arrived."

"Yeah?"

"Yeah." Then she went up on her toes, slanted her mouth against his and kissed him hard enough and long enough to make his knees shake and his blood boil. When she was finished, she stepped back, grinned up at him and grabbed the pizza box. "C'mon hero, let's eat."

He watched her walk down the hall toward the kitchen. His gaze dropped to the curve of her behind and everything in him tightened to the point of pain. But if she wanted a hero, then he'd be one. Even if it meant eating pizza when he'd rather be devouring *her.*

The next few days rushed past and the end of their first week together was looming. Megan's nerves were already stretched to their breaking point. She was hardly sleeping anymore. She worked all day at the estate, then came home at night to an empty house.

Since that night when they'd shared the bubble bath, the night he'd faced down Spencer at her side, Simon had kept himself at a distance. It was as if he was suddenly regretting their standing together as a team. Regretting making himself into her momentary hero.

He worked late every night and when he did come home and slip into their bed, he kept to his side of the vast mattress—driving her crazier than when he'd been sneaking up on her. He was up with the dawn and out of the house before she'd had her shower.

Megan threw a quick, anxious look at the closed front door, then turned and stalked down the long hallway, her heels clacking on the shining wooden floor.

"And now *this.*" Her stomach jittered and her mind raced. She'd been thinking all day. Thinking about what she'd seen, what she'd heard and what she'd done. Now, she had to think about how she was going to tell Simon.

"Darn it, he married me to *avoid* a scandal. Now, he's going to be dragged through one." Oh, she didn't doubt it for a minute. There was no way the Ashton family would be able to bury this one. Sooner or later, the news would leak and then the papers would be all over all of them.

Despite what her mother had tried to do.

"Oh, God." Megan stopped, rubbed her temples in a pitiful attempt to erase the headache that had been pounding behind her eyes all afternoon. But it wouldn't go away. Just as the memory of her own mother's callous cruelty wouldn't fade.

"Megan?"

She whirled around at the sound of Simon's voice. While she watched him, he stepped into the house, dropped his leather briefcase and walked toward her. "What's wrong?"

"Well," she muttered thickly, "guess I don't have much of a poker face, do I?"

"Not so much," he said, one corner of his mouth lifting, then falling again before it could become a real smile. "Tell me."

Here it was. She'd been waiting for him for what felt like forever and now that the time to talk to him was here, Megan felt her throat close up. She fought past it. "I don't even know where to start."

Taking her hand, he pulled her into the living room, off the foyer. The big room was dark and as he entered, he hit the light switch and puddles of golden lamplight spread across the room, chasing the shadows. Big overstuffed couches sat across from each other, with a wide oak coffee table between them. A cobalt-blue vase held a double bunch of white carnations and daisies that Megan had brought home only the day before. And somehow, looking at the simple cheerfulness of that bouquet made Megan feel even worse.

She pulled her hand free of Simon's and started pacing again. Somehow, she had to keep moving. As if trying to keep up with her racing mind—which, she told herself, was simply impossible.

"What the hell's going on, Megan?"

"Scandal for one," she blurted, unable to think of a gentle way of putting it.

"What—"

"I'm getting to it," she said and realized that now *she* was interrupting *him.* They'd come a long way. Shaking her head, she continued in a rush, "A woman came to the estate today. Her name's Anna Sheridan."

"And…?"

*"And,"* Megan repeated, still stalling. Stupid. Just say it. "She came to talk to my mother. About her nephew."

Simon frowned. "Your mother's nephew?"

"No, Anna's."

"Anna has a nephew."

"I just said that," she snapped, then held up one hand. "Sorry. Sorry. It's just that I've been thinking about this all afternoon and dreading telling you and at the same time *wanting* to tell you to, you know, get it out of the way, and now that you're here, I'm talking all around it and not saying a damn thing, which is really stupid, but I can't seem to stop and oh God, I need to draw a breath." She stopped, slapped one hand to her chest and felt the furious beating of her heart. Dragging one breath after another into her lungs, she locked her gaze with his as he came closer.

"Megan, what the hell is wrong?" Simon grabbed her shoulders the minute he was close enough and she felt the warmth of his hands right down to the bottom of what felt like a very cold soul.

She drew on that heat and held it close as she nodded. "I'm getting to it. Just not very efficiently. Okay, Anna Sheridan's nephew. Jack. A baby, really. Not even two yet. She had a picture. Cute little guy. Red hair. Green eyes. Great smile."

His lips twitched. "And you hate kids? The picture brought out a long-buried childhood trauma?"

He was joking. He was being nice. Damn it.

"No. No, it's nothing like that." She looked up at him so she could watch his eyes. "Little Jack is my half brother."

"What?"

"My *father*—" and she said the word with a bitterness that had been filling her mouth all afternoon "—had an affair. Probably should say *another* affair to be accurate. Though to be absolutely accurate," she muttered, "you'd probably need a scorecard. Anyway, he had an affair with Anna's sister Alyssa. Alyssa died after giving birth and Anna's been raising Jack—my father's son."

"Whoa."

"That about sums it up." Megan stepped away from him and swept one hand through her hair as she turned to stare out the front windows at the darkness beyond the glass. Instead, she saw her own reflection—and Simon's, standing right behind her. God. Was he wishing he'd married anyone but her? Probably. And who could blame him? "Anyway, Anna came to the estate looking for—I don't know. Money? Help? Recognition?"

"What happened?"

"About what you'd expect." She sighed and felt the cold, damp fingers of shame reach out for her again as she remembered. "Father wasn't home. But my mother was."

"And?"

She watched his face in the glass. Somehow it was easier talking to his reflection than to turn and face him. "And my mother practically threw her out. God." She closed her eyes, suddenly unable to face even the mirror image of Simon's face. But as soon as her eyes were closed, she saw her mother again. Saw the hard expression on her tight features and heard the withering tone of her voice.

Megan had long known that her mother wasn't a tower of warmth. But seeing her like that… "Her voice was like ice. She dismissed Anna Sheridan and the—and here I quote—'bastard' child. She told Anna that if she tried to come to the estate again, she'd bring charges of extortion against her."

"I don't even know what to say."

"That's okay," she said, finally opening her eyes. "Neither did I." She wrapped her arms around her own middle and finally forced herself to turn around and face her husband. "At first, all I could think was, *oh boy, another scandal. Won't Simon be pleased.* You married me to avoid scandal touching your family, your business."

"Life happens, Megan. Scandals blow over."

She cocked her head to one side and stared at him. "That's not what you said a week ago."

He shrugged. "I'm growing as a person?"

She laughed shortly and shook her head. "Fine. Maybe my father's scandals won't rub off on you. That's something to hope for, I guess."

"There's something else, Megan. Something that's bothering you more than worrying about tabloid reporters."

"Yeah," she said and met his smoky-gray eyes. "There is." And it had been torturing her all day. She could hardly say the words, but she had to. "Simon, I watched my mother turn that woman away and I couldn't take it. Just couldn't. Mother's never been what you'd call a really *warm* person. But somehow I never thought of her as completely cold, either. But today…" She shook her head and swallowed hard. "There was a part of me that was absolutely terrified that I could be like her. That one day I'd wake up and my voice would be just like hers. That I'd get swallowed up by the cold. That because she's my mother, I'm capable of that kind of callousness."

"You're not."

She choked out a laugh. "You said that too fast. You didn't think about it."

"Didn't have to."

Oh God, she wanted to believe him. But if a person could inherit the color of her parents' eyes or hair, couldn't she also inherit a cold heart? Or an empty soul? And why was she being so damned poetic?

She smiled wistfully. "I hope you're right. But because of my own fears, I caught up with Anna outside. I told her to go to Caroline Sheppard for help." She laughed shortly, harshly. "If ever there was a woman to help another with my father's cruelty, it would be Caroline."

"I'm not following."

"Not surprising. Caroline used to be married to my father. The estate originally belonged to her family. Then my father divorced her to marry my mother and—" She threw both hands up and let them slap against her sides again. "Now Caroline's married to Lucas Sheppard—"

"And they run Louret Vineyards," Simon put in, obviously catching on.

"Right," Megan said, "Ashton Estates and Winery's archenemy." Megan sighed, shook her head and said, "Listen to me. It sounds like a soap opera, doesn't it?"

He stepped up to her and settled both hands on her shoulders again, then slowly, he rubbed her upper arms as if trying to drive away a chill. "Families are complicated."

"Some more than others."

"What you did for Anna?" He dipped his head until he could look into her eyes. "That was kind, Megan."

"Maybe," she said and shook her head. "I hope Caroline can help her. But the bottom line is, I'm not even sure if I did it because it was the right thing to do or if I was trying to convince myself that I'm nicer than my mother. Sad, huh?" She looked away from his eyes, unable to meet that steady gray stare. "I just don't know. The only thing I do know is, what I did wasn't enough. That little boy is my father's son, damn it."

"You gave her more than your mother did."

"Yes, and now for my reward, I get to feel as though I've betrayed the family." Oh, and she didn't even want to think about how Spencer would take the news of her stepping in to help his mistress's sister and his illegitimate child. Oh yeah. That should be a fun scene.

On the other hand, she thought, since her father

still wasn't speaking to her, maybe she wouldn't hear anything from him at all.

"God, I'm a mess," she whispered and leaned her forehead on his chest.

Simon wrapped his arms around her and held her close, pressing her up against him. He'd stayed away from her these last few days, knowing that he was walking a razor's edge of control. And now tonight, he was holding her, and all he wanted to do was comfort. Thoughts of having her, sliding his body into hers, kissing her, tasting every square inch of her skin were fading, becoming more tender, more caring.

His heart ached for her, knowing how it felt to be torn between what you saw as your duty and what you knew to be right. He'd been doing his duty by his family ever since his father had died when Simon was seventeen. He'd been lucky enough to actually enjoy what he did for a living, but even if he'd hated it, he would have done it. He understood family loyalty. And knew what it had to have cost her to take a chance on ostracizing herself from those she loved by doing what she thought was right.

But damn he was proud of her.

"So," he said, enjoying the feel of her pressed up against him. "You pretty much had a crappy day."

She didn't even lift her head, but she did sigh heavily. "You could say that."

"You did good, Megan."

"I hope so," she admitted, then paused for a long

moment before asking, "What if I'm like my mother, Simon?" Her voice was a whisper and he almost missed the words because of the roar of his own heartbeat. "What if I'm that cold inside? That unfeeling?"

"You're not," he said, and willed her to believe. Grabbing her shoulders, he set her away from him enough that he could look into her eyes. "You're the warmest woman I've ever known. Stubborn, sometimes irritating," he added with a half smile, "but warm."

One eyebrow lifted. "Irritating?"

He grinned. "Figures that's the word you latched on to." Then his smile faded as he watched her worried gaze. "You did the right thing, Megan. You always do the right thing. You should trust your own instincts more."

She stared up at him and he felt the power of her green eyes slamming into him. He read the hope shining in their depths—and something else, too. A flash of heat, of desire, and his body jump-started into life.

"Trust my instincts?" she asked.

"They're good instincts," he said, and smoothed her hair back from her face with a tender touch. Her hair was soft and thick, and her skin as smooth and warm as sunlit glass.

He wanted her more than he'd ever wanted anything else in his life.

"Then I'll trust them. Starting right now." She

moved into him, went up on her toes and, wrapping her arms around his neck, she kissed him so long and hard and deep, Simon could have sworn his hair caught fire.

# Eight

The week wasn't officially over.

And Megan couldn't have cared less.

She wrapped her arms around Simon's neck and hung on while she kissed him hungrily, desperately. She poured everything she had into that kiss. Heart and soul, hunger and need, she let him know without words just how much she wanted him. Just how frantically she *needed* him.

A full minute later, she realized that he wasn't responding. He hadn't grabbed hold of her. Hadn't kissed her back. In fact, he was standing stiff and still, looking—and feeling—pretty much like a wax representation of Simon Pearce.

When that knowledge finally clicked into her brain, Megan broke the kiss and pulled her head back to look up at him. In the golden lamplight spilling throughout the living room, his smoke-gray eyes looked dark and dangerous. And her stomach jumped in reaction.

Her breath staggered in and out of her lungs. Her own heartbeat was deafening. Her blood pumped and parts of her body that had been sorely neglected over the last year were alert and ready to party.

But Simon was staring over her head at the wall behind her, tension etched into his features.

"Hello?" she said, her voice just a little ragged. "Anybody home?"

He swallowed hard and slowly lowered his gaze to hers. His pale, smoky-gray eyes were the color of thunderheads just before a huge summer storm. He didn't speak. He made no move to touch her. She just hung off his shoulders like a human cape.

"You know," Megan said, never taking her gaze from his, "that was a pretty good kiss you just missed."

"Didn't miss it. Trust me."

She tilted her head to one side and tightened her arms around his neck. "Uh-huh. So, why didn't you join me? Kissing's always more fun if two people do it."

He inhaled sharply, deeply, and through his starched white shirt, Megan felt the hard slam of his heart.

"The week's not up," he pointed out, through clenched teeth.

"What?" She'd heard him. She just couldn't believe it.

"I said, the week's not up till tomorrow." Simon's jaw muscle ticked. "We had a deal."

"So you're not going to do anything until the official end of the week."

"That was the deal."

He didn't sound happy about it, but he did sound determined. A part of Megan appreciated that. Nice to know that the man kept his word. However...

She combed her fingers through his hair, dragging her nails across his scalp and smiled to herself when he closed his eyes and gritted his teeth harder. "The thing is," she whispered, dropping small, nibbling kisses along his jawline between words, "I—don't—want—to—wait—"

He growled.

Actually *growled,* and something inside Megan turned over, then sat up and begged. She'd never wanted anyone as much as she did Simon Pearce right at that moment. Tall and strong and sure of himself. He wasn't the easiest man in the world to know, but she knew what she needed to know. He was honorable. Old-fashioned word, but a good sentiment. He wasn't afraid of her father. Also a good thing. He treated her like she had a brain—very sexy.

And he could do things to her body with the touch of a single finger that no other man had ever been able to do.

"Megan," he said, his voice just as stiff as the rest of him, "you had a crappy day. You're upset, you're vulnerable—"

"Simon…" She sighed and her breath brushed the base of his throat. The pulse point there jumped in response and she smiled to herself. "Stop being so damn *reasonable*."

She looked up at him.

He met her gaze and fires flared in the depths of his eyes. Fires that reached out for her and inflamed every square inch of her body.

*Wow.*

"Be sure," he ground out.

Megan smiled and shook her head. "If I get any more sure, I will officially be attacking you."

"Good point." He bent his head, took her mouth with his and gave her everything she'd given him only moments before.

Megan held on for dear life and jumped headfirst into a raging river of passion like she'd never known before. His mouth ravaged hers. His tongue tangled with hers, his arms came around her, pulling her so tightly to him, she was afraid she wouldn't be able to breathe—though a part of her wouldn't have cared, so long as he kept on kissing her.

Nothing mattered beyond Simon's mouth on hers, Simon's body pressed against her, the hunger stampeding through her system.

A week ago, she wouldn't have believed that she'd

feel like this. A week ago, she'd looked at Simon as a virtual stranger—and perhaps the solution to the problem of Willie Jackson.

Now, tonight, he was so much more.

He'd stood alongside her, making them a team. He'd comforted her, laughed with her, and annoyed her. He was in her mind all the time and in her dreams every night.

His hands swept up and down her back, holding, touching, exploring and all Megan could think was, she wanted his hands on her skin. She wanted to feel the heat of him, feel the imprint of each of his fingertips as he stroked her and drove her body higher and higher.

Simon tore his mouth from hers and dropped his head to the curve of her neck. His mouth, his teeth, his lips worked against her throat and chills raced up and down her spine. "Simon…"

"No more talking," he muttered against her neck. "Just feeling."

"Right," she said, agreeing with a sharp nod. "Feel. Want to feel more."

"Good. Very good." His mouth dipped a bit lower, nestling on the pulse point at the base of her throat and she tipped her head to one side, hoping he'd stay there for a minute or two—or forever.

His mouth was a wonder.

"Want you," he murmured, his words coming in an agonized whisper, strangling with need.

"Me too, want you, too," she agreed, scraping her hands up and down his back, wishing she could just blink and have his suit coat and shirt gone.

"Now."

"Oh yeah," Megan said, mind whirling into oblivion. She couldn't think. Didn't want to think. Just wanted him. "Now."

His hands came around to her front, swept up between their bodies and as he continued to nibble on her neck, his fingers made quick work of the buttons lining the front of her pale-green silk blouse.

"Faster," she said, amazed at the fire burning within her.

To please them both, he grabbed the edges of her blouse and gave them a yank, shooting the remaining buttons into every corner of the room. He tugged the fabric off her shoulders and down her arms and then all that stood between Megan and Simon's hands on her body was her bra. He made quick work of that, too, and in an instant, his hands were cupping her. His thumbs and forefingers tweaked and teased her nipples, setting off a chain reaction inside her that had Megan gasping for air and choking out encouragement.

"Your mouth," she whispered. "I want your mouth on me."

"Yes." One word, ground out through a tight throat and Simon fought through the cloudy haze of passion obscuring every thought but need. Had to have her. Had been thinking of nothing but this for days, what seemed like years.

Every night, she lay within an arm's reach and was still untouchable. Every day, he tried to fill his thoughts with work, with the very thing that had been his focus most of his life. Instead, Megan was there with him, every moment, every hour. Thoughts of her plagued him, infuriated him, tortured him.

He'd told himself only that morning that it would all be over tomorrow. That once they'd slept together, once he'd buried himself inside her, tasted all she was and all she promised, then he would be satisfied. Then his world would slip back onto the tracks and all would be as it should be.

Now though, with her in his grasp, her warm sighs and eager hands only served to feed the need, not satisfy it.

Dropping to his knees in front of her, he dragged his hands down the length of her body. When he hit the waistband of her skirt, he unzipped the fabric and pushed it down her legs, dragging her panties, a fragile scrap of black lace, along with it. And then she was there, in front of him, naked and willing and just as hungry as he.

Her knees wobbled and he caught her, hands on her bottom, steadying her, even while drawing her legs apart gently, carefully, despite the urgent need inside him.

"Simon, I want—"

"I want, too," he whispered brokenly. "I want *you*."

Then he leaned toward her and covered her center with his mouth. He tasted her as she gasped and swayed in his grasp. His tongue teased her center, flicking gently over the sensitive nub of flesh at her core.

*"Simon!"* Her hands fisted in his hair and she locked her knees even as she leaned into him, holding him to her as if half-afraid he would stop.

He couldn't stop.

Wouldn't stop.

Not until he felt her body dissolve. Not until he'd tasted her pleasure and experienced her surrender. Again and again, he swiped her warm flesh with his tongue, driving her higher and faster with every stroke. His grip on her behind tightened, her sobbing gasps urging him on until she cried his name and swayed violently in his grasp.

As the last of the tremors rocked her, he eased her onto the floor, the soft fabric of the oriental rug cushioning them both. She lay, spent, staring up at him as he quickly tore off his own clothes and then leaned over her.

"Simon, that was…" She smiled and lifted both hands weakly, as if unable to come up with just the right word.

He did it for her.

"…just the beginning." Then he parted her

thighs with his knee, positioned himself between her legs and slid into her slick heat with a groan of satisfaction.

Her body closed around him, holding him tightly and Simon's vision blurred.

She reached up for him, taking his face between her palms and pulling him down for a kiss. Her lips parted and her tongue touched his, tangling, dancing intimately in an imitation of his body moving in and out of hers.

Over and over, he felt the rush of desire take him by the throat and squeeze. He felt the wild fulfillment of being inside her. Of touching her so deeply.

He broke their kiss and looked down into her summer-green eyes and lost himself in the clear, soft depths of them. Her hands slid up and down his back. She lifted her legs and rocked her hips, moving with him in a rhythm that was as old as time and as new as a breath.

And when her tremors began again, Simon dipped his head for another kiss and kept them joined completely as they chased each other into the light.

Megan's back hurt.

She was pretty sure she had rug burn on her behind.

Her legs were cramping.

And if he tried to move, she'd have to kill him.

Suddenly, he did move, trying to pull free of her

body, but she held him still after releasing one soft gasp. "Don't," she warned, clamping her arms tightly around him and holding him to her. "Don't move."

He chuckled shortly and his warm breath dusted the curve of her neck. "If I don't, I'll smash you."

"I'm sturdier than I look," she assured him, closing her eyes to better enjoy the sensation of his body moving within hers again.

He propped himself up on his elbows and stared down into her face. "Wouldn't you rather move upstairs?" he asked, a half smile curving his mouth. "You know? To an actual bed?"

"Mmm…" She rocked her hips and nearly smiled herself when he hissed in a breath. Good to know she wasn't the only one going up in flames around here. "Later."

"Right," he said, punctuating the single word with a long, slow kiss that ended with him nibbling on her bottom lip.

"That was really amazing, Simon," she said when her mouth was free again. "I mean, *amazing.*"

"Yeah," he admitted, "that about covers it."

Megan felt loose and limber and, okay, a little achy, but in a good way. Her body was humming, her mind was in neutral and for now, that's just how she wanted it.

"Think we could do that again?"

He grinned. "Is that a direct challenge?"

"Does it have to be?" She rocked her hips again,

and reached down with one hand to stroke the curve of his backside.

He sucked in a gulp of air and pushed his body hard against hers. "Nope."

"Oh, boy." She held on as he rolled over onto his back, somehow keeping their bodies locked together despite the quick move. And then she was straddling him, and his hands, his wonderful, clever hands with their long, sensitive fingers, were on her breasts, tugging, teasing, cupping and stroking.

Megan sat up straight and arched her back, moving into his touch even as she took his body deeper within her own. She felt the hard, solid strength of him, pushing higher, higher until she would have sworn he'd actually touched her soul.

He groaned and she opened her eyes to watch him as she took him. Power filled her and it was a delicious and heady drug. She moved on him, rocking back and forth, then swiveling her hips in a slow, tight circle that set off incredible sensations deep inside her. In reaction, he lifted his hips, arching higher into her body, as if he couldn't be deep enough, close enough.

"Megan—" His hands tightened on her breasts, fingers delicately squeezing her nipples, and she reached to cover his hands with her own.

His eyes glazed over and his mouth worked as he fought for control. Then his gaze shifted to their joined hands and he groaned tightly. Megan watched his inner battle and smiled to know that she could push such a strong man to the brink of powerlessness.

"Enough," he muttered and tried to move, to shift her to the carpet so he could roll atop her and set their pace.

"Not even close," she whispered, lifting her arms high above her head as she rocked atop him. "Let me, Simon, let me take you this time."

"You're killing me, Megan," he managed to say, though every word sounded as though it had cost him dearly.

She shook her head and smiled as she rode him, lifting her body, then lowering it again, taking him deeply, then releasing him in a slow, languorous dance that drove them both to the edge of desperation. Her body tensed, a sense of anticipation climbing within, marking each second with breathless wonder. Sensation after sensation coiled within and every time she moved on him, she soared a little higher.

She leaned back then, arching her spine and tipping her head back, shifting his body's position inside her until he was pressing on exactly the right spot to send her hurtling into space.

"Simon," she whispered, never breaking pace, never slowing as she continued her erotic dance atop his body. "Simon, I feel—"

"I feel it, too," he murmured, and his voice was a sigh in the roar of her own blood.

As she moved on him, he dropped one hand to the

joining of their bodies and stroked her with a single fingertip. Again and again, he caressed her until she was trembling, aching for the release she knew was hanging just out of her reach.

She gasped, she fought for air, fought to hang on to the rising climb of her body's tension. She wanted that climax and at the same time, didn't want this moment to end. She wanted to trap them somehow in time—right here, right now. To hold this position for eternity—this one exquisite moment just before the tremendous release she felt getting nearer.

Simon's body bucked beneath her as he exploded, she heard him shout her name and still, he touched her, never stopping, never easing until all at once, she saw stars erupt behind her closed eyelids and felt the world rise up and then dissolve around her.

And she wondered…who had taken *whom?*

Two hours later, they were sprawled across the continent of their bed. The remains of a hastily grabbed snack lay scattered across the sheets and a half-empty bottle of wine was being passed back and forth between them.

Megan put her mouth on the bottle and tipped it back, taking a long drink of the smooth, tart wine. Then grinning, she said, in the stuffiest voice she could manage, "An impudent wine, with the grace of maturity and just the slightest touch of adolescence."

Simon's mouth twitched as he took the bottle from

her and had a long drink himself. "Tart, yet sweet. Bold, but not too sassy."

"Not bad," Megan said, nodding. "You've been to wine tastings before."

"A few," he admitted, leaning against the pillows stacked against the carved headboard. He lifted one knee and rested his forearm atop it. "None as casual as this one, though."

"Casual?" Megan asked and crawled across the mattress until she was right next to him. She couldn't stand to stay on the opposite side of the wide mattress. She needed to touch him, to trail her fingertips across his skin, to smooth her hands over his whole body, to feel him get hard for her again.

*Oh boy.*

She collapsed in a heap over his broad and really exceptionally well muscled chest. Every bone in her body felt like an overcooked noodle. She'd never been so limp with satisfaction—and so hungry for more. "I think we're dressed very appropriately."

He ran his palm over her behind, squeezing, stroking, and Megan damn near purred as she moved beneath his touch. Honestly, who would have guessed that stiff and stern Simon Pearce had so many hidden talents? The man was a wizard. He'd done things to her body tonight that she hadn't even dreamed of. He'd taken her higher and faster than she'd ever been before.

And, she wanted him again.

Her heart rolled over in her chest.

More, she wanted *him* to want *her.*

"If we keep this up, we'll kill each other," Simon mused, his hand still caressing her bottom with long, lazy strokes.

Megan didn't want to move. Didn't want to risk him stopping touching her. But she chanced a look over her shoulder at him. "There are worse ways to go."

"True." His eyes darkened. Even in the pale, soft light thrown from the lamp on the nightstand, she could see his features tighten. She watched hunger flash in his eyes and she swallowed hard.

Megan's stomach pitched and swirled.

Her mouth went dry and certain other parts of her body dampened in anticipation. Oh, she'd had absolutely no idea what she was getting herself into when she'd agreed to a temporary marriage to Simon Pearce.

And if she *had* known?

"I have to have you again," Simon whispered, his voice a soft growl in the shadows. As he spoke, his hand slipped down between her legs, his fingers delving into her heat.

Megan parted her thighs for him then slid her eyes closed and concentrated on the incredible sensations building within her again.

If she'd known?

She wouldn't have waited a week.

# Nine

**"I** don't care if the Peabody Corporation withdraws from the deal." Simon leaned back in his desk chair and stared at his assistant.

Dave Healy shook his head, blinked, then tipped his left ear toward his boss. "Excuse me? Would you mind repeating that?"

"Funny." Wryly, Simon smiled. "I mean it, Dave. If the old man wants to pull out of this deal, that's his business. Let him find someone else willing to put up with his antiquated ideas about building a company."

Morning sunlight slanted through the bank of windows behind Simon's desk and sketched out tall panels of light on the steel-gray carpet. Dave Healy stood in one of those slashes of gold, clutching a manila file folder.

"Never thought I'd hear you say that."

"To tell you the truth, neither did I." Simon straightened up again, planting both elbows on the gleaming black surface of his desk. Even while Dave talked, Simon's brain wandered. Something he'd noticed happening more and more often lately—since Megan had entered his life.

The last few days had been hard on her. The papers were full of the latest Ashton scandal and Megan fretted over every headline. Her father's illegitimate child was news and every reporter in the state was constantly looking for a fresh angle from which to attack.

He knew she was more worried for him and for his business than she was about herself, and though he appreciated it, he kept trying to tell her she didn't have to be.

True, scandals were bad for business, especially when dealing with people like Manfred Peabody—an old coot who would have been much more comfortable living out his life in Victorian England. But it wasn't as if this scandal actually touched his family. Pearce Industries was safe. Spencer Ashton was an ass, but it wasn't going to affect Simon. Except, of course, for the effect the old goat was having on Megan.

And even as that thought slid through his mind, he realized that just a couple of weeks ago, he couldn't have imagined feeling that way. But things had changed now. Megan was his wife and he wasn't going to let old man Peabody—or anyone else for that matter—insinuate that she'd done anything wrong just by being born an Ashton.

Megan.

Lately, everything came down to Megan. He hadn't expected this "temporary" marriage to be anything more than a convenience. But it was quickly becoming so much more than that.

She was creeping into every corner of his life. And that was something he hadn't counted on.

"Simon!"

"Huh?" He blinked and looked up at Dave. The man was shaking his head and grinning.

"Where the hell is the steely focus and single-minded concentration that makes Simon Pearce a man to be feared across the mortal globe?"

A short, sharp laugh shot from his throat as he stood up and shoved his hands into his pants pockets. Shrugging his shoulders, he looked at Dave and admitted, "Hell if I know."

His old friend nodded thoughtfully. "It's about time."

"What's that supposed to mean?"

"It means," Dave said, stuffing the file folder under his left arm, "that you've been living for this company for too long."

Simon frowned, but didn't argue. Hard to when the man was absolutely right.

"You've always been eat-sleep-breathe work," Dave went on. "That's not healthy."

He snorted and walked around the edge of his desk. On the far wall, a sterling-silver clock ticked off the hours until he could go home again. Until he could be with Megan. Damn it, he *had* lost his focus. He eased himself down and perched on the edge of his desk. "Healthy," he said. "This from a man who thinks of French fries as vegetables."

Dave grinned. "My point is," he said, ignoring that last little jab, "you're allowed a life, Simon, and you haven't been getting one."

He frowned. "I have a life."

"The company doesn't count."

"It's all that ever has counted," Simon said softly.

"Until now," Dave pointed out. He took a step closer and slapped Simon's shoulder. "Megan's good for you, Simon," he said. "I'm glad you've got her."

"Temporarily. Our deal was for a temporary marriage."

Dave laughed and turned for the door leading into his own office. He opened the door, then paused to look back at his boss. "Aren't you the man who's always believed that deals were born to be renegotiated?"

Even after Dave left, his words hung in the air, like a…what? Challenge? Suggestion?

Simon's fingers curled around the edge of the cold black desk and he stared hard at the clock on the wall while his mind raced. Did his marriage really have to remain temporary? Did he *want* more from Megan?

He didn't know.

All he could really be sure of was that he wanted Megan now.

Tomorrow was too far away to be worried about.

And yesterday was too empty to remember.


"Charlotte, I think I'm going nuts."

Megan stalked across the living room of the small guest cottage where her cousin Charlotte lived. The rooms were tiny, but beautifully kept with warm, polished wood floors and beamed ceilings. A tiny one-story structure, it was built of stone and wood, and when she was a girl, Megan had believed it to be a storybook cottage, complete with fairies and pixies and everything else a little girl dreamed of.

Now, it was simply her cousin's home. Charlotte Ashton had never cared for living at the main house, preferring her own company in this cozy place. Besides, the greenhouses were just behind the cottage, keeping things easy for the woman who created beautiful floral arrangements for the events held on the estate.

"You're wearing a hole in the floor," Charlotte said quietly.

"Sorry, it's just—" Megan stopped and threw her hands wide.

"You have to pace when you're anxious. I know."

Charlotte sat curled up on a dark-rose sofa, a velvet throw pillow clutched to her chest. Her long, straight black hair hung down well past her shoulders and looked like a silk cape she'd tossed on for effect. She was tiny and patient and soft-spoken—all the things Megan wasn't.

Perhaps that's why they got along so well.

Megan took a deep breath, blew it out, then dropped onto a dark green side chair. The overstuffed cushion rose up around her like a comforting hug. "The newspapers are full of Father and his latest—I don't even know what to call it."

"Episode?" Charlotte offered.

"As good a word as any." Megan shook her head, then reached up and pushed one stray lock of blond hair behind her ear. "Reporters are hovering outside the gates, attacking every car that leaves, phoning the estate, pestering customers who are just here for a wine tasting." She paused for breath. "And yesterday, one of the TV crews actually made a sixteen-year-old cry at her own birthday party." She cringed, re-membering how the young girl and her friends were chased down the drive by an overeager reporter and his cameraman. "Mother won't talk about it, Trace keeps his head buried in work, Paige pretends every-thing is normal, Father refuses to say anything—even told me himself this morning that since I had chosen to turn on him, taking my husband's side over his, that he owed me nothing. No explanations, nothing."

She cringed inwardly, remembering that scene in her father's estate office only that morning and wondered how she could ever have imagined that Spencer might want her opinion. Then she shook it all off and said, "And Simon…"

"What about Simon?"

"I don't know," Megan admitted and added silently that that was what she was most worried about. Simon hadn't said anything about this latest disaster of her father's. Not since that first night when she'd broken it to him and then they'd… Her body went hot for one gloriously amazing moment, and then that feeling drained away completely. "God, Charlotte, I don't know what to do. What *can* I do? This is all just a mess."

Charlotte's features hardened. "You know I'm no fan of your father's, Megan."

"I know and maybe that's why I came to see you. Everyone at the main house is walking on tiptoe around the place as if leery of stepping out of line. But how can we?" she demanded of no one. "When Father's the one who keeps moving that line?"

"You act as though you're surprised by all of this," Charlotte said and leaned forward to pick up her cup of tea off the small round coffee table.

"And I shouldn't be, you mean."

Charlotte shrugged and took a sip of her tea. "I can't blame you for not wanting to see the truth about your own father. But Megan, I've known the truth for years. The man cannot be trusted. At all."

Megan told herself she should be insulted. She should feel the urge to leap up and defend her father. She always had before. She'd spent so many years trying to explain away Spencer's behavior, his attitude, his treatment of others, that it was almost second nature to her now.

But the sad fact was, she couldn't do it anymore. She couldn't even manage to convince *herself* that Spencer was the kind of father she'd always wished him to be. In the last two weeks, it was as if blinders had suddenly been ripped off her eyes and she saw him not as she'd wanted him to be, but as he really was.

A man who had sneaked around on every wife he'd ever had. A man who made babies and then walked away. A man who hadn't spoken to her in anything but monosyllables since the night he'd accused her of defying him. No, there was no defense for Spencer.

Not from her.

Not anymore.

"God," she whispered. "You're right." An admission she'd never have said out loud before now. She might have thought it, but she never would have allowed herself to be disloyal enough to say it.

The last two weeks had apparently changed more than her love life. Megan smiled to herself as she realized that, somehow, she'd stopped looking for her father's approval. Maybe it was just that she'd finally acknowledged that it would never happen.

But maybe it was something more.

Maybe it was that she'd finally discovered that having her father approve of her wasn't as important as approving of *herself.* She straightened slightly in the chair and thought about that for a moment. A small ribbon of satisfaction snaked through her system and Megan smiled.

Charlotte looked at her over the rim of her teacup and her dark-brown eyes glimmered in the late afternoon sunshine spearing through the wide window. "You're going to be all right, aren't you?"

"You know?" Megan said slowly, "I think I am."

"I'm glad."

"Thanks."

"Glad for me, too, because now that you've finally accepted some of the truths about your father, I can tell you something."

Her voice was so serious, her features suddenly drawn into lines of tension, Megan instinctively leaned toward her. "What is it? Is something wrong?"

"That's just it. I don't know."

"Charlotte…"

She took a deep breath, then another swallow of her tea, as if to gather the strength to say what she had to say. "You know how your father's always insisted that my mother died?"

"Yeah." Charlotte's parents were David, Spencer's younger brother, and Mary Little Dove Ashton, a Sioux. When David and Mary died, Spencer brought their children, Walker and Charlotte, to live at the estate.

"I don't believe it," Charlotte said softly.

"You think your mother's still alive?"

"I have to find out," she said. "I have to know one way or the other. Walker thinks I'm crazy, but Megan, something inside me is telling me not to believe your father's version of the story."

Would her father really have lied about Mary Little Dove's death? Megan wondered. And a moment later, she admitted that yes, if it had served his purposes at the time, he would have.

Reaching one hand across the table, Megan waited until her cousin took it in a firm grip. Then, their hands joined in solidarity, Megan said, "Find out, Charlotte. And if you need any help, just call."

Phoebe Pearce smiled at her daughter-in-law and stood up in welcome as Megan made her way through the crowded restaurant.

Her nerves were skittering badly, but Ashtons learned at an early age how to hide anxiety. Megan plastered a broad smile on her face and leaned down to give the tiny woman a quick kiss on the cheek. "It was so nice of you to invite me to dinner."

"Nonsense." Phoebe waved one hand as she took her seat again, then deftly flicked her pearl-gray napkin across the lap of her stunning forest-green silk suit. "When I learned that Simon would be working late tonight, I just knew it would be a good chance for the two of us to get in a little girl talk."

Girl talk.

How bad could it be?

Phoebe seemed very nice, but Megan was still feeling the pangs of guilt for marrying the woman's son under false pretenses. At least though, she knew that Simon had kept his word and explained the real situation to his mother.

"Would you like a drink, dear?"

"Wine would be nice," Megan said.

"Of course." Phoebe smiled again and motioned to a waiter hovering nearby. "I should have known an Ashton would prefer wine." She spoke quickly to the waiter and then turned back to Megan. "I've ordered a lovely chardonnay I think you'll enjoy."

"Thank you." Megan wished it were sitting in front of her right now, since her throat was dry and those nerves were doing a mambo up and down her spine. When those nerves hit her throat, she started talking, as if to assure herself that she was just dandy. "I do prefer chardonnay and you know, everyone thinks the grapes will be wonderful this season."

"I didn't realize that your family bottled chardonnay."

"Oh, we don't," Megan said quickly, falling into talk of grapes with gratitude. "But we do grow the grapes and then use them in our cuvée."

"Of course. It must be fascinating, the making of wine."

"Well, to be honest, I'm not much involved with the actual winery." Her brother Trace was the estate manager and could probably have told Phoebe everything she'd ever wanted to know about wine and more. But Megan and Paige, beyond helping with the harvests as children, had nothing at all to do with the actual winery. "I run the events at the estate and—"

"Oh I know, dear, but still. You're there. A part of it all. The vineyards, being at the mercy of the weather, all very earthy and exciting."

Megan smiled, despite the interruption. "Not very exciting when you're a child and expected to help out at harvest time. Then you just get muscle cramps and blisters on your fingers."

While Megan talked about everything and nothing, the waiter arrived and poured their wine. Then, after giving them a moment to study the menu, he took their orders and disappeared again.

Megan sucked in a great gulp of air and told herself to stop babbling. In an attempt to get her runaway mouth under control, she let her gaze sweep around the crowded restaurant. Each of the dozen or more tables were covered with crisp white linens and boasted a small, round vase bursting with spring flowers. The soft, silky sounds of classical music drifted from the snow-white piano in the corner of the room as a young woman in a pale pink gown delicately stroked the keys.

Everything was beautiful.

Phoebe was very nice.

So why did Megan feel so on edge?

"I wanted to talk to you privately, Megan," the older woman said.

*This is why,* Megan thought, wondering what her mother-in-law had in mind. "Yes?"

"About Simon." The older woman smiled and her pale-gray eyes shone with good humor. "As his mother, I simply have to congratulate you and tell you how happy I am about your marriage."

"Really?"

"The change in him these past couple of weeks is nothing short of extraordinary."

"I'm sorry?" Megan hadn't expected this at all. In fact, given all the gossip surrounding her father at the moment, she wouldn't have been surprised if Phoebe had demanded that this temporary attachment to her son end immediately. And she couldn't have blamed the woman for it, either.

Phoebe reached out and covered Megan's hand with one of hers. "My dear, you've done wonders for him."

Confused, Megan simply stared at her.

"I had lunch with him only yesterday and he was…relaxed in a way I've never known him to be. He smiled. He enjoyed himself." She smiled again and winked. "He didn't rush me through lunch so that he could return to work."

Megan shook her head. "I don't think that's because of anything I—"

"Nonsense." Phoebe smiled at the waiter as he set their dishes in front of them. When he was gone, she spoke up again. "A man who's happy at home becomes happy in every area of his life."

"Phoebe," Megan said quickly, before she could be interrupted again, "I know Simon told you the truth about our marriage."

"Certainly."

"Then you know that we're not—"

"In love?" Phoebe finished for her and Megan gritted her teeth at yet another interruption. "I wouldn't be so sure, my dear."

She tried to argue the point, but didn't get far. "Really, Phoebe…"

"Megan," the woman said, "I've known my son a lot longer than you have. And I can tell you that I have never seen him like this before. It's as if he's found something he hadn't known he was missing. And that something, my dear, is *you.*"

Megan's heart lurched a little, but she didn't allow herself to actually believe Phoebe. The woman may think she could see love when she looked at Megan and Simon. But all she was really seeing was good chemistry.

Right?

A marriage that had begun with a business deal couldn't really turn into something more, could it? Neither of them had been looking for love when they'd stumbled into this marriage of convenience. Neither of them had so much as mentioned the word.

Now that Phoebe had though, it was as if all bets were off. *Love.* Was it possible? Was it something she should even be considering? Her insides dipped and spun and her heartbeat stuttered irregularly. Megan's brain whirled as she tried to think about a year from now and saying goodbye to Simon.

Pain, sharp and swift, jabbed at her and she swallowed hard. If, after two weeks, the thought of leaving Simon was painful, how much worse would it be after a whole year?

*Oh, God.*

Phoebe was probably wrong about Simon's feelings—after all, he'd shown no signs of wanting anything more from Megan than he had when he'd proposed.

But, the older woman had been dead on target about one thing.

Somehow, over the last two weeks, Megan Ashton Pearce had fallen in love with her husband.

# Ten

The third week of Megan's marriage was radically different from the first two.

Those first couple of weeks, she and Simon had had his big house all to themselves. They'd had a little time to get used to each other. To get used to the idea of being married—and then they'd had time for other things. *Lots* of other things.

That first night of lovemaking had opened the door to more amazing nights than Megan would have thought possible. They'd made love in practically every room—even once on the stairs. They'd taken long showers together and shared cozy, intimate meals together in the kitchen. Just the two of them in that big house, they'd never worried about privacy or having someone overhear their conversations.

But that was all different now.

Now, their full-time cook was ensconced in the kitchen, so there were no midnight refrigerator raids. There were maids in and out of every room in the place, so there were no make-out sessions on the sofas. There was a full-time gardener, so there was no more lovemaking under the trees in the backyard.

"Not that there was much chance of that now anyway," Megan muttered. After all, Simon was spending more and more time at work and less and less time with *her*. He left home early in the morning and often wasn't home until ten or later. It was as if he were trying to avoid being at the house—or rather, being with *her*.

Megan wrapped her arms around her middle and stalked around the confines of her bedroom. The house, despite being full of people now, felt empty when Simon wasn't there.

Despite what his mother Phoebe had had to say at the restaurant the week before, Megan was sure that her new husband was regretting this temporary marriage. Her heart ached just a little, but she put a stop to that really fast. She had no right to be hurt—or disappointed.

This marriage was just what it had started out to be. A convenience. A pretense, with good sex. No one had said anything about happily ever after. No one had mentioned the word "love." No one, including her, had anticipated their feelings changing.

She stopped at the wide windows overlooking the backyard and the hill that rolled on down through the valley. Plopping down onto the wide cushioned window seat, she stared out through the glass at the darkness beyond. She hadn't bothered to turn any lights on in the bedroom. But there was a low fire burning in the hearth, more for atmosphere than warmth, and the flames were reflected in the glass. The sky overhead shone with pinpricks of light and the moon slanted a spotlight down onto the manicured gardens below.

Resting her head against the wall, she let her gaze wander the darkness while her mind raced over too many thoughts at once. The newspapers were still hounding the Ashton family—apparently there were no fresh scandals anywhere else to knock them off the front pages yet. Spencer had closed himself off from everyone, refusing to talk about Alyssa Sheridan or the boy. Simon kept assuring Megan that her father's troubles didn't bother him—but how could she believe that?

"It's your own fault," she murmured, tracing one finger across the cool glass. "Who the hell told you to fall in love with your husband?"

Stupid.

Simon wasn't interested in love. He'd made that clear the day they'd been so hastily married. All he'd been looking for was a way to keep his family and his company free of scandal. A one-year marriage. Strictly business.

But now scandal had found them anyway and Simon…damn it, she could tell. He was distancing himself from her. She felt it. Even when they were in the same bed, even when he was holding her or sliding his body into hers, she felt him pull away. And she didn't know how to stop it—or even if she should try.

So she couldn't very well add to the wonderful blend of misery by admitting she'd gone and fallen in love with him.

"Oh yeah," Megan said, turning around to slide off the cushioned bench, "my life's a party."

"Am I invited?"

Her head snapped up and her gaze shot to the open doorway of the bedroom. Simon stood there, jacket hooked on an index finger and flung over one shoulder, his tie opened and the top button of his dress shirt undone. He looked tired, a little harassed and too damn good.

She swallowed hard and wondered if she'd ever get used to the simple joy of just looking at him. God, he could turn her insides to a gooey puddle with one glance out of those fog-gray eyes. No point in letting him know that, though.

She cleared her throat. "What?"

"You said your life's a party." Simon echoed her words as he stepped into the room and closed the door behind him. "I was just wondering if I was invited or not."

How could he not know that *he* was the party?

And how was she going to be able to live with him for a whole year and *not* eventually blurt out the truth about how she felt? Oh, she wished she were a better liar. Or even a better actress.

She sucked in a gulp of air, told her nerves to shut the hell up and forced a smile. She'd just have to find a way to keep the fact that she loved him her own little secret.

Now that he was home though, thoughts and worries rushed out of her mind, leaving her body hungry and her heart trembling. He might not love her, but even as he mentally distanced himself from her, she knew he still *wanted* her. So for the moment, she'd let go of tomorrow and concentrate on tonight.

"Sure you're invited," she said and walked toward him, her bare feet silent on the thick, plush carpet. Slipping out of her robe, she let it slide down her arms to hit the floor, leaving her wearing only a silk pale-green camisole and matching panties. The cool night air brushed her skin, but she didn't feel it. How could she ever feel cold when Simon's heated gaze was on her?

One dark eyebrow lifted as he watched her approach. "Just what kind of party is this?"

Even his voice was rich and dark and sexy. The deep rumbles of it rolled through her, setting her nerve endings on fire. Firelight cast dancing shadows across his features and flickered in his eyes.

"It's a 'you're late and I missed you' party."

He frowned slightly, tossed his jacket to the foot of the bed. "Didn't mean to be this late, but—"

Megan shook her head, reached up and covered his mouth with her fingertips. "Doesn't matter. You're here now."

One corner of his mouth lifted and something flashed in his eyes. "Just in time for the party?"

"You're the guest of honor, actually."

"Yeah?" he asked, allowing her to pull him over to the wide continent of their bed. "What do I win?"

"Me." Megan unbuttoned his shirt, dragged the end of his tie free and tugged it off of him. Then scraping her hands along his arms, she pushed his shirt down and off, then slid the palms of her hands across his chest. He hissed a breath of air through gritted teeth and she smiled to herself, loving the knowledge that in this, at least, she could touch him.

She couldn't tell him she loved him.

But she could show him.

Dipping her head, she pressed her mouth to the base of his throat and sighed against him as his hands came up to stroke her skin beneath the silk of her camisole.

"You feel so good," he whispered, his breath brushing the top of her head, ruffling her hair. "You always feel so damn good."

"I'm glad," she said, her words muffled as she continued to kiss him, moving, shifting, until she tasted first one of his hard, flat nipples and then the other.

He groaned, clutched her to him and fell back onto the bed.

She lifted her head and looked down at him. His features tight and drawn, his eyes were now the color of night smoke, dark with need, glittering with desire. If she couldn't have his love, she would at least claim his need.

For now.

For this one moment, Simon Pearce needed her. Wanted her.

And that was all that mattered.

"I don't know what you're doing to me," he admitted, reaching up to stroke her hair back from her face, over her shoulder. His voice was rough, as if he were forcing the words out past a tight throat. "But I think about you all the damn time."

That was something, wasn't it? He thought about her. He wanted her. It wasn't love, but it was something.

"I'm glad of that, too."

"I have to have you, Megan."

"I'm right here." She dropped a kiss onto his mouth, tugging at his bottom lip with her teeth.

"Not close enough," he groaned and flipped her over until she lay beneath him. "Not nearly close enough." In seconds, he had her naked and writhing beneath him. His hands, his fingers, his mouth, were everywhere. He touched her and flames erupted. He kissed her and the inferno started. He tasted her and explosions shattered through her body.

Megan twisted on the sheets, hungry. Hungrier for him now than she'd been that first time. She couldn't seem to have enough of him. Every time only made her want him more. Was this love? she wondered. This crashing, thundering need to be with him, under him, a part of him?

And if it was, how would she ever live without it?

Then her thoughts shuddered to a halt as he moved away from her long enough to strip out of his own clothes. She watched him in the firelight, and fed her own hunger. She'd never expected to feel so much. To feel so deeply. And now that she did, she was sure she'd never be able to survive living with him and knowing that he didn't feel it, too.

Then he was back, covering her body with his, kissing her, sighing into her mouth, wiping every thought from her mind. The brush of his skin against hers was magic. His hands slid over her body and she lifted into his touch, needing more, wanting more. Wanting all of him.

Everything but Simon fell away.

Everything but this moment disappeared.

"This is crazy," he murmured against her throat as he positioned himself between her thighs. "Your scent stays with me always. Your sighs are in my dreams. Your face is in front of me all the time. I hear your voice when you're not even there."

She smiled and clutched his words to her, holding them as close as she held him. Closer even, since she tucked them away into her heart, to warm her later, when reality crashed back down on her. When he was gone and she was alone and trying to remind herself that love had not been a part of this bargain.

"Take me, Simon," she whispered. "Take all of me."

She arched into him, lifting her hips in silent plea.

He caught her hands with his and planted them on the mattress on either side of her head. And leaning in for a kiss, he pushed himself into her depths while claiming her mouth. Their tongues mated, danced, as their bodies moved in a rhythm older than time. As the first tremors rocked her body, Megan heard him whisper her name before he took the leap and fell with her.

Later, as she lay beside him in the firelit darkness, she watched him sleep, and wondered how she would survive losing him.

"The new contracts are being messengered over." Dave stood in front of Simon's desk, waiting for a reply.

"Fine. Let me know when they arrive."

"Hey," Dave said, "curb the enthusiasm. Not safe for your heart."

Simon sighed and leaned back in his chair. Forcing a grim smile, he asked, "Better?"

"God no."

"It's the best I can do."

"What the hell's going on, Simon?"

Good question, he thought. But what was the an-

swer? He spent his days trying to stay busy enough
to keep thoughts of Megan at bay—then he spent his
nights trying to climb inside her body. Where was the
logic in that? Where was the control? He used to be
in charge, damn it.

"I don't know. Miserable mood, that's all." He sat
up again, grabbed his silver pen and dragged a sheaf of
papers toward him. "Your best bet is to stay far away."

Naturally, Dave plopped down into the closest
chair, stretched out his legs in front of him and said,
"Talk."

Simon snorted. "About what?"

"Megan, of course."

"This has nothing to do with Megan."

"Right." Dave actually laughed as he shook his head.

"Who're you? Mr. Advice to the lovelorn?"

"Hell no, but I'm as close as you've got."

"Sad but true." Simon leaned back in his chair
again, tossed his pen to the desk top and then shoved
one hand through his hair with enough strength to
snatch himself bald. "Fine. She's making me nuts."

"This is a good thing."

"For you maybe, not for me."

"Why?"

"Because I don't *do* love, damn it."

"Who said anything about love?" Dave's grin was
huge and his damn eyes were practically twinkling.

"Swear to God, if you laugh, I'll clean your
clock."

"No laughing. Just enjoying."

"Good for a man to have friends who can relish his pain."

Dave spread his arms wide. "I do what I can."

"Trust me, you've done enough." Simon pushed back from the desk, stood up and started pacing. Hell, he felt as though if he didn't move, he just might start unspooling. Was that even a word? "This is all your fault," he muttered.

"Okay, how did I get into this?"

"You're the one who said I should have a life. That Megan was good for me."

"Guilty as charged."

Shaking his head, Simon walked faster, as though he were trying to escape the thoughts plaguing him, but there was just no way he could run fast enough—or far enough. "I started thinking and damn it, that wasn't a good thing either. Because the more I thought about it, the more I realized that I'm in love with her."

"That's great!" Dave jumped up to congratulate him, but Simon just sneered.

"It wasn't in my plan."

"Screw the plan, Simon," Dave said. "You finally found somebody and I think it's great."

"Oh yeah, *great*." Simon stopped dead and glared at his best friend. "I don't want to be in love. Love is chaos. And I don't like chaos."

"Well, welcome to the world, Simon." Dave

leaned back against the desk. "Nobody's in control all the damn time."

"*I* am," he argued, then scowled again. "At least I used to be."

Dave chuckled.

Simon's gaze narrowed on him. "And I will be again."

"Oh, this I gotta hear."

"Fine. Listen up." Crossing the room toward his oldest friend, he talked while he walked. "I figured it out this morning. All I have to do is make Megan admit she loves me first. *Then* I regain control."

"You're nuts."

"It makes sense." Warming to the whole idea now that he'd said it out loud, Simon went on. "Think about it. First one to speak loses power—if it's true in business, then why shouldn't it be true in love?"

"Because love isn't supposed to be about one-upmanship."

"Right. Remember why you surprised Peggy with the week's stay in Hawaii last summer?"

Dave stiffened. "That's different."

"You said it was so that *you'd* be the one making the romantic move. So you'd get the brownie points."

Rubbing the back of his neck, Dave said, "There's a flaw in there somewhere."

"No there's not," Simon said, walking back around his desk to sit down again. "I've pulled off way more hostile takeovers than this. You'll see. I love Megan. I know she loves me, too." He stopped, thought about it, then nodded. "Yeah. She really does. All I have to do is somehow get her to admit it before I do. How hard can it be?"

Dave scowled at him. "Why does that have the ring of 'famous last words'?"

"He's our father, Megan," Paige said, striding across the reception hall floor. "Of course I'm going to support him. You should be, too."

"I tried that. You know I did." Megan shook her head and followed her younger sister, heels clicking noisily on the glossy marble floor. She knew Paige wasn't listening to her. Didn't *want* to hear her. And Megan was sorry for it. She and her sister had always been close. And now that the scandal over baby Jack had stirred things up in the family, it was as if everyone were taking sides—and she and her sister were on opposite sides of the fence.

"Honestly," Paige muttered darkly. "To listen to you and Trace, anyone would think Father was some kind of monster."

Megan's headache pounded in time with her steps. Trace. Her older brother. At least she had the satisfaction of knowing that he felt the same way she did.

As she walked, Megan's careful gaze swept the hall, absently checking that everything was ready for the wedding reception to be held there the following day. Round tables, each sitting ten people, dotted the floor. Pale peach linen tablecloths were spread over them and the matching slipcovered chairs were pulled up close. Vases atop every table waited for the peach roses that would arrive in the morning. Along the far wall, several smaller round tables marched in a long line, seating for the bridal party. And on the opposite end of the hall, a wide area was set apart for dancing.

A soft breeze drifted through the open veranda doors on either side of the hall and carried the scent of roses with it.

Everything was as it should be. Whatever else might be going on around Megan, she'd managed to at least keep her work on track. As she acknowledged that thought, she told herself it wasn't hard to work, when that's all you really did anymore.

Paige stopped at the wide double doors and turned to face her as she approached. Megan looked at her sister's stubborn features and wanted to sigh. She might have finally accepted that their father was not the man she wished he was, but clearly Paige still had hopes. And she wasn't alone, either.

Their mother, Lilah, refused to even discuss the matter of Spencer's illegitimate son. More than that though, she refused to believe that anything at all was wrong. She blindly insisted that her life was as perfect as she'd always claimed it to be.

Cousin Charlotte, of course, had never liked or trusted Megan's father, but Charlotte's brother

Walker was Spencer's right-hand man. Together, Walker and Paige kept trying to insist that everything would work out. That the man they were so busy defending didn't really *need* defending at all.

And Megan was tired of arguing the point.

"Okay," she said as she came up close to her sister. "I'm sorry. We won't talk about Father anymore, all right?"

Paige blew out a breath, then smiled and laid one hand on Megan's forearm. "Thanks. And you'll see. Father will explain everything and the rumors will fade away as soon as the newspapers find someone new to pick on."

"I hope you're right," Megan said, though she didn't hold out much hope. She had a feeling that as far as her father was concerned, things were going to get worse—not better. She only hoped that Paige wouldn't be too crushed when she was finally forced to see her father for what he really was.

# Eleven

Over the next few days, Megan felt…jumpy. It was as if she were waiting for the other shoe to drop.

The sun warm on her back, she continued on her walk through the vineyard. She loved the smell of the vines and the freshly turned earth. She loved walking the long, orderly rows of just-budding vines because it gave her a sense of connection—of continuity. And yet, even being out here wasn't enough to dispel a vague sensation of impending doom.

"Okay," she murmured to herself, after checking to make sure no one was standing around watching the crazy woman talk to no one, "you're getting a little dramatic, Megan. Dial it down a notch or two."

But how could she?

Even avoiding reading the newspapers and watching television, she was aware of the trouble her family was going through. And she was more than aware of just who was responsible for this mess.

Her father.

"Hey, talking to yourself is not a good sign."

Megan turned around so quickly, her low-heeled black pumps caught on a grapevine root and she rocked unsteadily until her big brother grabbed her elbow and held on. "Thanks," she said, "but next time, if you're going to scare me, wait until I'm barefoot at least."

Trace grinned and Megan couldn't help smiling back. The man was just gorgeous. Six feet tall with an athletic build, eyes as green as her own and light brown hair, when he smiled, women lined up in front of him just to melt.

"Wasn't worried about you," he quipped. "But take it easy on the grapes, huh?" That said, he went down on one knee to inspect the knobby, gnarled vine as if checking to make sure Megan hadn't done any damage.

"Nice to know I come in second to a vine."

"Hey, if we could make cuvée by squeezing your pretty head, it might be a different story." He stood up, reached out and touched the tip of her nose with his index finger.

Megan felt a rush of love for the big brother she'd

always adored—even when he was stealing her toys and hiding them just for the heck of it. He'd always been there for her. Always ready to listen, or to give advice—even if she didn't want it.

Which today, she suddenly realized, she really did. Maybe that's why she'd walked down to the vineyard in the first place. Maybe her subconscious had steered her in Trace's direction because she'd known deep in her heart that she just had to talk to someone who would understand.

"Why so serious all of a sudden?" he asked, then stopped and nodded. "Ah. You saw the morning paper."

"I stopped reading the paper almost two weeks ago."

He winced. "Then you don't know."

"Oh, God." For the first time in her life, Megan knew absolutely what the phrase about experiencing *a sinking sensation* actually meant. "What?"

Draping one arm around her shoulder, Trace started walking and Megan fell into step beside him.

"One of those eager-beaver reporters got tired of rehashing the same old story about our new little half brother—"

"And…" Oh man, she didn't want to ask. Didn't want to know. But how could she *not* know?

*"And,"* Trace said on a long sigh of either frustration or disgust, it was hard to tell which, "it seems there are more skeletons dancing in Father's closet than anyone guessed at."

Megan stopped short and looked up at him. "Tell me."

Frowning, he shifted his gaze from her to the wide sweep of the vineyard. And slowly, just like always, his features relaxed, despite whatever he was thinking. Being out in the field was like that for Trace. "You won't like it."

"Goes without saying."

He nodded. "Seems our father was married *before* he married Caroline Lattimer Sheppard. To a woman named Sally Barnett."

Megan blinked. "Okay, surprising maybe, but how does that compare to his having a child and trying to hide it?"

"Because, little sister," Trace said, letting his gaze slide back to hers, "Father never bothered to get a divorce from his first wife."

It was a good thing Trace still had a grip on her shoulders because Megan swayed with the impact of his words as surely as she would have if someone had punched her in the stomach. *Never got a divorce?* "How is that possible? What kind of person does that?"

A muscle in Trace's hard jaw twitched. "I think you already know the answer to that one, Megan."

"Oh my God," she whispered, then leaned into her brother, drawing on his stalwart, dependable strength. "If he didn't divorce his first wife, then his marriage to Caroline wasn't legal, so his divorce and marriage to *our* mother wasn't legal either and—"

"Right," Trace muttered thickly, giving her a brief hard squeeze. "Which means," he continued, "this vineyard might be going back to the Sheppard family—through Caroline."

"It'll be turned over to Louret Vineyards?" she whispered, suddenly understanding the magnitude of what she'd just learned. "You're right. Father got this vineyard in the divorce settlement. But if he and Caroline were never actually married..."

"...Then there would be no divorce—or settlement."

"God, Trace, we could lose the estate? The vineyard? The winery?"

"That about covers it." He started walking again and Megan kept pace, despite her wobbly knees.

"I'm an idiot."

"Interesting segue," Trace said and there was a touch of humor in his voice now.

Megan dropped her head to his shoulder. "I came out here, looking for you, I guess. I wanted to ask your advice."

"Always happy to tell other people what to do."

"I know," she said and sighed softly. "Now though..."

"What's wrong?"

"It's—Trace, I don't know what to do about Simon."

"Your husband? What're you talking about?"

She stopped and he looked down at her, all concern. "I was worried about the scandal surrounding baby

Jack and how it would affect Simon and his business. Now there's *this*. I just don't know what to do. I don't want to drag Simon down with the rest of us."

"He's your husband, Megan."

"I know." This wouldn't work. She couldn't ask Trace if he thought she should stay with Simon or leave him unless she explained the whole weird story of their marriage. And she wasn't prepared to do that. So quickly, she changed the subject. "There's more. I'm worried about Paige, too. She still trusts Father and now with this…it's really going to hit her hard."

Trace's features tightened and old pain shimmered in his eyes. "She'll have to find out, Megan. She'll have to see it for herself, just like we did. Like I did."

"Trace?"

He shook his head. "Let's just say that I learned five years ago just how treacherous our father can be."

"What happened?" Five years? She'd still been in college. What could have happened that she didn't know about?

"I'm not going into it, Megan. It's over." He blew out a breath. "But I will tell you that Spencer Ashton screwed me over. Cost me the only woman I've ever loved."

"Oh, Trace," she said softly, reaching up to cup her brother's cheek in her palm. An ache settled in her heart and she wished there was something she could do, or say, that would help. But judging by the stark, raw pain in his eyes, there was nothing.

He sighed again and gave her a half smile. "I don't know what's going on with you and your husband, Meg. But I will tell you to trust yourself. And if you have to make a choice between family and your heart, choose your heart."

Sounded simple. Now all she had to do was figure out what her choice would be. Megan wanted to scream. Her father's greed and blind ambition had brought them all to this point—and now it would probably cost her the future she might have had with Simon.

"Mrs. Pearce—a comment for our readers?"

"Over here, honey, smile for the camera!"

"Hey, how's it feel to know your father made you a bastard?"

Megan gritted her teeth and kept her gaze focused straight ahead. She'd thought that once she left the Ashton estate behind, she'd be free of the reporters. But no. There were at least a dozen of them, complete with news vans and cameras, staked out at the foot of the driveway leading to Simon's house.

They were going to ruin him. Ruin a man who'd made the mistake of marrying an Ashton. *Don't look,* she warned herself. Don't give them the satisfaction of seeing her cry. Of seeing her pound the steering wheel in frustration.

"Hey, what's your new hubby think of dear old dad?" another reporter shouted as he skittered sideways, bending down to look into the driver's side window. "Bet he's sorry he ever hooked up with you, huh?"

She slammed on the brake, jerking the car to a stop. Whipping her head to the left, she glared at the big-mouthed, rude, obnoxious reporter and snapped, "You leave my husband out of this."

The reporter, a short bald man with eager eyes and a smarmy grin shook his head. "No can do, honey. Simon Pearce is big news, too. And when he's linked to the Ashton family high jinks, well, that sells papers."

Cameras flashed, microphones were jammed at her, reporters and TV crews jostled for position and Megan could have sworn she felt the earth beneath her shudder and shake.

Simon.

Big news.

Linked to the Ashtons.

God.

"So," the reporter asked, taking her stunned silence for a decision to talk to the press, "what about it? What's Simon 'Squeaky Clean' Pearce have to say about the family embarrassment?"

She inhaled sharply, thought about telling them all to go to hell, then pictured *that* little confrontation on the front page and the six o'clock news and changed her mind. "No comment," she snapped and stepped on the gas.

It did her heart good to see the reporters skip back

out of the way of her tires. But that flush of pleasure only lasted a second or two, then the lead weight of reality settled in the pit of her stomach and she knew it wasn't going anywhere.

It was time to make that choice she and Trace had talked about.

By the time Simon got home, it was after ten and he felt as though he'd done ten rounds with a heavyweight champion. Dropping his briefcase to the floor, he leaned back against the closed front door and closed his eyes. Damn, it had been a nightmare day.

Reporters had buzzed around his offices, futilely hoping for an exclusive interview. The phones had rung off the hook and Dave had spent most of the day soothing Pearce Industries' clients and snarling at people demanding comments on Spencer Ashton's latest mess. Plus, there was an encampment of reporters parked at the edge of his driveway.

Simon should have been furious.

His company was under fire. He personally was being stalked by reporters. His family was being drawn into what promised to be an ugly situation played out on the front pages of every newspaper in the country.

And yet…

All he'd been able to think about all day was how this was affecting Megan. At the thought of her, he pushed away from the wall. "Megan?"

His shout seemed to echo in the stillness. There was no sign of anyone in the big house. It was as if Megan and his employees had all disappeared.

Scowling at that mental image, he stalked across the hall toward the staircase and the bedrooms above. Damn, she was probably alone and crying. He wanted to go and tell Spencer Ashton just what an ass he was for hurting his daughter. He wanted to find Megan's dragons and slay them. He wanted to—damn it, he wanted to love her. Wanted her to love him.

He should never have come up with that stupid plan to wait her out. To make her confess her love first. He should have told her as soon as he'd recognized just what a lucky bastard he was. Should have told her that he wanted this marriage to be real.

His footsteps sounded overly loud in the quiet and he tried to shrug off the sensation of abandonment that clung to the house. Taking the stairs two at a time, he hit the landing at a dead run and raced down the carpeted hallway toward the master bedroom. He pushed the door open, and felt his heart drop to his toes when he didn't see her. Then he rushed to the bathroom. No sign of Megan. Anywhere.

His gaze dropped to the gleaming blue-green tiles and noticed that her wide array of creams and lotions, her hairbrush, even her toothbrush, were missing. His heart stopped momentarily. "Doesn't mean anything," he muttered. "Not a thing." She wouldn't leave. Not without a word.

Not without telling him, damn it.

But anxiety chewed on him, nibbling at the corners of his heart, tearing at his soul with dread as he turned and headed back out into the hallway. It was a big house, he told himself. She could be anywhere. "Megan?"

He swallowed hard as he took the stairs going down, just as quickly as he had going up. By the time he hit the foyer again, Simon's insides were churning and his brain was racing.

Then he saw her. Standing beside the open front door, looking at him with a world of pain in her eyes and a steely determination on her face.

"Megan." He started toward her, but she backed up, shaking her head.

"Don't, Simon. Don't make this harder. On either of us."

Harder? What could be harder than that feeling of mindless despair when he couldn't find her?

"What're you talking about?" His blood rushed through his veins, clouding his vision, thundering inside his head.

"I'm going."

"Going where?" Two words. All he could manage.

"Doesn't matter," she said and swallowed hard. Her summer-green eyes filled with tears she frantically blinked away. "I'm sorry. Sorry about all of this. The mess with my father—you being involved. I'm sorry."

*Damn it.* He took a step closer, but she kept pace, backing up until she was now on the porch, with the night behind her. He was too wary to try to get closer. "You don't have anything to be sorry about."

She laughed, but there was no humor in it, only regret. "I'm an Ashton," she reminded him wryly. "Apparently, that's more than enough reason to be sorry."

"This isn't about you, Megan," Simon said and wished to hell she'd come back into the house. So they could talk.

She shook her head again and lifted her chin in a defiant tilt he recognized. "I'm packed."

Panic rushed through him again, this time making his knees weak. "Packed? Why?"

"I'm leaving, Simon. I have to. You saw the reporters out there." When he opened his mouth to argue, she cut him off. "They're not going to be leaving anytime soon. This thing with my father is only going to get worse and I'm not going to bring your family down with mine. I won't do it, Simon."

"Don't you think you should let me decide that?"

"No. Decision's made. We had an agreement when we got married. No scandals, remember?" She gave him another smile and a wrenching pain slammed through him as he read goodbye in her eyes.

"Megan, don't."

"I'll sign the divorce papers as soon as they're ready." She turned away and started walking. "Goodbye Simon."

He couldn't move. He wanted to chase her down and drag her back. Hold her tightly enough that she couldn't walk away from him again. But he suddenly felt as though he were made of stone. He couldn't force life into his limbs. He stood there like a man who'd been cut in two and didn't know enough to fall down.

The night swallowed her while he stood alone in the big house that had her memory stamped all over it.

His plan had failed. She hadn't said she loved him first, so she'd left, never knowing how much *he* loved *her.*

Not knowing that by leaving, she was killing him.

# Twelve

Hiding out on the estate wasn't exactly the brainiest idea Megan had ever had. After all, it was like trying to hide from sharks by diving off the Great Barrier Reef.

The Ashton estate was like a medieval castle under siege. No one but family was allowed in, all tours and events had been canceled. Reporters still clustered outside the gates. Freshly hired security guards kept them at bay, but that didn't mean they'd stop trying to get an interview or a picture or a comment from anyone going in or out of the main gate.

She'd come home after leaving Simon two days before because she couldn't think of anywhere else to go. Pitiful. But the only place she wanted to be was with Simon. And since she couldn't do that, what did it matter where she went?

At least here, on the estate, she was protected enough that she didn't have to deal with the media. Charlotte had welcomed her into the cottage, since Megan couldn't bear the thought of moving back into her old rooms in the family home—just the idea of having to deal with her parents right now gave her cold chills. Charlotte though, busy with her plants and flowers in the greenhouse, gave Megan plenty of space and time to herself.

Now, all she had to do was try to find a way to keep herself busy until thoughts of Simon faded away. Shouldn't be more than twenty or thirty years. How hard could it be?

She flopped back into one of the comfy, squishy chairs in the cottage living room. "Oh, God…"

"Why don't you come and help me in the greenhouse?" Charlotte walked into the room and stopped beside her. "Take your mind off of things."

Megan sighed and patted her cousin's hand. "Thanks, but we both know I suck at the whole Mother Nature thing. In ten minutes, you'd be able to *hear* your plants screaming for help. I'd just be getting in your way."

Charlotte smiled. "I don't mind."

"And I appreciate it," Megan said, looking up at her cousin. Her features were serene, but her dark eyes shone with worry and Megan appreciated her cousin's unspoken concern. "But I'm just lousy company, Charlotte. I think I'll take a walk or something."

The other woman shrugged and gave her a half smile. "Or, you could take a drive. Back to your own house. To your husband."

Megan's heart twisted and the rippling pain of it shot throughout her body with lightning-like precision. "I can't. I can't drag him through this mess."

Charlotte cocked her head to one side and studied her for a long moment before asking, "What makes you think you would have to drag him? Maybe you should give him the option of deciding for himself."

"Say I did," Megan countered, "say he decided to stay with me and because of that decision, he lost clients and his family was hurt by what's going on with *our* family. Then what? How long before he resented me? How long before he couldn't stand the sight of me?" She shook her head. "No thanks. My way's better. Quicker."

"Megan…"

She lifted one hand and rubbed at the ache in the dead center of her chest, but it didn't help. Nothing would help. Ever. She'd be walking through the rest of her life like this. In pain. Might as well get used to it. Megan stood up, reached out and gave her cousin a brief, hard hug, then pulled back. "I appreciate what you're trying to do, really."

"But butt out?" Charlotte asked, smiling.

Megan managed to briefly return the smile. "Gently put, but yeah."

"Okay," her cousin said and started for the back door that would lead her across a tidy garden to the greenhouse, "but remember, if you change your mind, I'm here if you want to talk."

Alone, Megan headed for the front door of the cottage and stepped out into a splash of sunshine that dappled the stone pathway with light spearing through the sheltering leaves of the nearby trees. She wandered along the path, then stepped off into the lush green grass and let her gaze sweep wide across the manicured lawn. Rolling hills of rich green stretched out in front of her like swatches of velvet. Well tended flower beds were a riot of color—purple, yellow, deep red—and their combined scents filled the air.

Yet for all the beauty surrounding her, Megan felt as though she were locked in a dark room. Worse, deep inside, she knew there was no way out. This was a lose-lose situation all the way around.

Simon had spent the last forty-eight hours trying to find a way into the Ashton estate. But it was like trying to sneak into Fort Knox. The security guards out front weren't letting anyone through, damn it. Every time he tried to phone, he was told politely, but firmly, that the Ashton family was not accepting calls at the moment.

"Not even from husbands," he muttered grimly and stared down the burliest of the guards, who'd planted himself in front of Simon's car like a cement pylon with sunglasses. His fists squeezed tightly around the steering wheel and he forced himself to fight for calm. Not easy, when all he wanted to do was push his way past the guards, stomp onto the estate and turn the place upside down if he had to, to find Megan.

Megan.

God.

He scrubbed one hand across his face and felt the scrape of whiskers against his palm. Hell, he hadn't even shaved. Hadn't been able to think about anything or anyone but his wife, since the moment she'd walked out of the house two days ago.

He should have chased her down. But by the time he'd been able to coax his nearly paralyzed body to move, she'd driven off into the night and he'd missed his chance. Missed the chance to tell her he loved her. Needed her. Would not live without her and she'd just have to learn to live with it.

"Great. Good plan," he told himself, disgusted. "Sure to win the heart of any woman. Start telling her what to do."

He was in bad shape. But he'd have been much worse off if he hadn't gotten a telephone call just an hour ago. Charlotte, Megan's cousin, had phoned him and asked just one question. "Do you love her?"

As soon as he'd convinced her, Charlotte had invited him to the estate and assured him that she'd get him past the guards. All he had to do now was be patient. It wasn't easy though. Not when he was so close.

Finally, one of the guards nodded at him, opened the gate and allowed Simon's car to pass through. Anticipation rattled around inside him as he followed the drive, headed for the small stone cottage Charlotte had described. *What if Megan wouldn't listen?*

He pushed that thought aside.

She *had* to listen.

Had to believe.

With her back against the gnarled surface of a tree trunk, Megan stared at the vineyards, stretching far into the distance. Plucking a blade of grass from the blanket beneath her, she shredded it methodically and let her mind race where it would. Naturally, it went straight to Simon. His image rose up in front of her. His scent wafted around her, competing with the strong earthy scent of the garden. And everything inside her yearned to go to him. To throw herself into his arms and feel him holding her close.

How would she ever bear to be without him?

"You're not an easy woman to talk to."

Her eyes flew open and she shifted a quick, disbelieving look over her shoulder. Simon. Here. And not looking very pleased about it. His features were grim and shadowed by at least a day's growth of whiskers. He wore jeans, a wrinkled white pullover and black sneakers. As he came closer, she could see the spark of something dark and dangerous in his eyes. She pushed herself to her feet, determined to have this confrontation on equal footing.

"We don't have anything to talk about," she said softly, letting her gaze feast on him. Had it really only been two days? It felt like weeks, months, since she'd last seen him, touched him.

"That's what you think."

"Simon—"

"You had your say, Megan." He stopped a foot away from her.

So close and yet still so very far away. Her heart ached, and her fingers itched to smooth his rough jaw. He looked as frustrated and exhausted as she felt. "Simon…"

"Uh-uh. My turn." He kept a tight grip on a folded newspaper in his right fist. "Two nights ago, you didn't give me a chance to talk. You just laid down your rules and walked out."

"It had to be that way," she argued and felt the first sting of tears fill her eyes. But she refused to let them fall. She'd cried enough over the last couple of days and wouldn't do it again now. In front of him. At least, she thought, maintain a *little* dignity.

"According to you."

"According to our *deal,*" she reminded him. "Remember? The no-scandal thing?" She choked out a harsh laugh that scraped her throat and hurt her heart. "Well look around, Simon. Scandal Central."

"You think I care?" Simon stepped in closer, until she was no more than a breath away. Damn it, he'd been wanting nothing more than to talk to her for two long days. Now that he was here, with her right in front of him, talking about doing the right thing and scandals, he just wanted to grab her and shake her. And then kiss her senseless. "Do you really think I give a good damn what's happening to your family right now?"

She sucked in a breath and drew her head back.

He shook his head in frustration. "That came out wrong. Of course I care. But only to the extent of what it's doing to you. I don't want to see you hurt, Megan."

"Then you'd better leave now," she whispered.

He heard the crack in her voice and everything in him tightened protectively. He didn't want to see her hurt, but he was doing a damn fine job of it himself at the moment.

Sucking in a long, deep gulp of air, he blew it out again in a rush and admitted, "I'm just a little nuts today."

"I'm getting that."

His lips quirked. "Megan, when you left—"

"I had to—"

"—it almost killed me."

"Oh, Simon."

"I can't lose you, Megan." He rubbed the back of his neck viciously. "*Won't* lose you." Then he handed her the newspaper. "Here. Read this."

"What're you…?"

"Just read it. Then we'll talk."

As her gaze dropped to the front page of the *Times,* Simon kept his own gaze fixed on her face. He saw every emotion as it flashed across her features. Read wonder and then surprise and then pleasure in her eyes and he hoped it would be enough.

"I don't understand," she whispered, never lifting her gaze to him.

"Then read it out loud. Maybe it'll help."

She nodded tightly.

"Pearce Speaks Out. Simon Pearce, in an exclusive interview, stated that his wife, Megan Ashton Pearce, is the most important person in the world to him. He assured this reporter that he and his wife will continue to support her family in this difficult time."

"Clear enough?" he asked, and this time, his voice was gentle, as if he were trying to coax a wild deer close.

She took a shuddering breath and looked up at him. Her beautiful green eyes awash with tears, he took hope from the tremulous smile curving her mouth. "Oh Simon, I don't know what to say."

Frustrated and just a little worried, Simon blurted, "Don't you get it, Megan? I *love* you. I should have told you before. But I was an idiot. I wanted to make *you* say it first, so I wouldn't lose control of the situation." He laughed sharply, shortly. "That was so stupid, because the minute I said 'I do' to you Megan, I lost control. And I don't even want it anymore. All I want is you."

"Simon, I love you, too. But I didn't want to tell you because we'd agreed to a temporary marriage."

"Nothing temporary about us, Megan. Not a damn thing. If I had another hundred years to love you, it still wouldn't be enough."

She lifted one hand to cup his cheek. "I only left because I didn't want you to be hurt by what was happening with my family."

He caught her hand with his, then turned his face and planted a kiss in the center of her palm. "The only way I can be hurt is if you leave me."

"Then you're destined for a lifetime of happiness, Simon," she said as she stepped into the circle of his arms and held on tight. "Because I'm not going anywhere."

His arms wrapped around her like a vise, pressing her close. "Damn right you're not."

She laughed and the music of it filled his soul, and Simon sent a quick, heartfelt thanks to whichever Fate had granted him a second chance. How had he ever lived without her? Still smiling, he lifted his head and looked down at her. "You know, it's a good thing you're coming home with me."

"Really?" She tipped her head to one side and teased, "Why's that?"

"Because, Mrs. Pearce, have you stopped to think at all that you could be pregnant?"

Megan's smile faded, her eyes went wide and her mouth dropped open. "Oh for heaven's sake." She went limp in his grasp. "With everything that's gone on in the last few weeks, can you believe I never even thought about it?"

He hadn't either. Not until the night she'd left him alone in that too-big house with nothing to keep him company but thoughts of what might have been. And in those first lonely hours, he'd been forced to acknowledge that when he'd lost Megan, he'd lost all hope for a future. For a family. With the only woman he'd ever loved.

Now though, he had her back in his life, in his heart. And he swore silently that he'd never do anything to risk what they'd found together. A swell of love for her rushed through him with the force of a tidal wave that surged to every corner of his soul. Staring down into her summer-green eyes, he felt himself hoping they'd have a house full of children and that each of them would have her eyes.

"Yeah well," he said, pausing to drop a kiss onto the tip of her nose, "I've been thinking about it for the last couple of days—"

"And…?" She watched him, those fabulous eyes of hers bright with happiness.

"And," he repeated, still dumbstruck with the force of his love for her, "I'm hoping you are."

"Really?"

"Really," Simon confessed. "But if you're not, we'll just have to try harder."

"Sounds like a lot of work," she said, shaking her head solemnly, despite the smile tugging at the corners of her mouth.

"Lady," he said, lifting her off her feet, "ask anybody. Simon Pearce *loves* hard work."

And he swung her in circles until they collapsed with laughter, tangling together in the shade of the oak tree, lying in the cool, damp grass and sharing a promise of the future with a kiss.

\* \* \* \* \*

# THE CRENSHAWS OF TEXAS

Brothers bound by blood
and the land they call home!

# DOUBLE IDENTITY

(Silhouette Desire #1646,
available April 2005)

## by Annette Broadrick

Undercover agent Jude Crenshaw
had only gotten involved with
Carina Patterson for the sake of
cracking a smuggling case against
her brothers. But close quarters soon
led to a shared attraction, and Jude
could only hope his double identity
wouldn't break both their hearts.

*Available at your
favorite retail outlet.*

If you enjoyed what you just read,
then we've got an offer you can't resist!

# Take 2 bestselling
# love stories FREE!

# Plus get a FREE surprise gift!

**Clip this page and mail it to Silhouette Reader Service™**

| **IN U.S.A.** | **IN CANADA** |
|---|---|
| 3010 Walden Ave. | P.O. Box 609 |
| P.O. Box 1867 | Fort Erie, Ontario |
| Buffalo, N.Y. 14240-1867 | L2A 5X3 |

**YES!** Please send me 2 free Silhouette Desire® novels and my free surprise gift. After receiving them, if I don't wish to receive anymore, I can return the shipping statement marked cancel. If I don't cancel, I will receive 6 brand-new novels every month, before they're available in stores! In the U.S.A., bill me at the bargain price of $3.80 plus 25¢ shipping and handling per book and applicable sales tax, if any*. In Canada, bill me at the bargain price of $4.47 plus 25¢ shipping and handling per book and applicable taxes**. That's the complete price and a savings of at least 10% off the cover prices—what a great deal! I understand that accepting the 2 free books and gift places me under no obligation ever to buy any books. I can always return a shipment and cancel at any time. Even if I never buy another book from Silhouette, the 2 free books and gift are mine to keep forever.

225 SDN DZ9F
326 SDN DZ9G

| | | |
|---|---|---|
| Name | (PLEASE PRINT) | |
| Address | Apt.# | |
| City | State/Prov. | Zip/Postal Code |

***Not valid to current Silhouette Desire® subscribers.***

***Want to try two free books from another series?***
***Call 1-800-873-8635 or visit www.morefreebooks.com.***

\* Terms and prices subject to change without notice. Sales tax applicable in N.Y.
\*\* Canadian residents will be charged applicable provincial taxes and GST.
   All orders subject to approval. Offer limited to one per household.
   ® are registered trademarks owned and used by the trademark owner and or its licensee.

DES04R                                              ©2004 Harlequin Enterprises Limited

# COMING NEXT MONTH

### #1645 JUST A TASTE—Bronwyn Jameson
*Dynasties: The Ashtons*

When Jillian Ashton's arrogant husband died, it wasn't long before she found a man who treated her right—*really* right. Problem was, Seth—a tall, dark and handsome hunk—was her late husband's brother. She'd planned on just a taste of his tender touch, but was left wanting more....

### #1646 DOUBLE IDENTITY—Annette Broadrick
*The Crenshaws of Texas*

Undercover agent Jude Crenshaw only meant to attract Carina Patterson for the sake of cracking a case against her brothers. But when close quarters turned his business into their pleasure, Jude could only hope his double identity wouldn't turn their new union into two broken hearts.

### #1647 RULES OF ATTRACTION—Susan Crosby
*Behind Closed Doors*

P.I. Quinn Gerard was following a suspected accomplice—or so he thought. When the sexy bombshell turned out to be her twin sister, Claire, Quinn no longer had to watch her every move. But he couldn't seem to take his eyes off her! Could Quinn convince Claire to bend the rules and give in to their mutual attraction?

### #1648 WHEN THE EARTH MOVES—Roxanne St. Claire

After Jo Ellen Tremaine's best friend died during an earthquake, she was determined to adopt her friend's baby girl. But first she needed the permission of the girl's stunningly sexy uncle—big-shot attorney Cameron McGrath. Cameron always had a weakness for wildly attractive women, but neither was prepared for the aftershocks of this seismic shift....

### #1649 BEYOND BUSINESS—Rochelle Alers
*The Blackstones of Virginia*

Blackstone Farms owner Sheldon Blackstone couldn't help but be enraptured by his newly hired assistant, Renee Williams. Little did he know she was pregnant with her ex's baby. Renee was totally taken by this older man, but could she convince him to make her—and her child—his forever?

### #1650 SLEEPING ARRANGEMENTS—Amy Jo Cousins

The terms of the will were clear: in order to gain her inheritance Addy Tyler needed to be married. Enter the one man she never dreamed would become her groom of convenience—Spencer Reed. Their marriage was supposed to be hands-off, but their sleeping arrangements changed everything!

SDCNM0305